omega

edited by roger elwood

A FAWCETT GOLD MEDAL BOOK

Fawcett Publications, Inc., Greenwich, Connecticut

contents

omega

running around

barry n. malzberg

I travel back in time seventy years to the bucolic and gentle year of 1903, where I meet my grandfather as a young man and kill him with a .32 caliber Smith & Wesson revolver. By so doing, of course, I assume that I have settled the difficulties of the instant situation, but when I return in my self-invented, secret time machine—I work in a laboratory in the cellar and refuse to patent any of my devices since I believe that modern corporations are irretrievably corrupt and will steal anything—I find my wife in her accustomed position in the living room, her arms folded, a bitter expression on her face.

"Now we won't have any of that," she says, referring to my travels in time, with which, of course, she is familiar (I would not have her misconstruing my jaunts as adulterous quests or expeditions to the bar, and thus keep her abreast of my findings), "there are the same bills to pay, the oilman is knocking down the door, the credit bureau has called three times this afternoon, and I'm tired of lying and this has got to come to an end. Edgar, you must face your responsibilities."

Edgar. My name is Edgar. My wife's name, on the other hand, is Betty and in a moment of passion some years ago I dragged myself, to my infinite regret, from my laboratory to court and marry her. We have two children, Richard and Helen, fraternal twins, eight years old. This was a dreadful mistake. Not the children, I mean—children are inevitable in any marriage. The marriage itself was a dreadful mistake. Inventing a time-travel machine had been my hobby and I should have left it at that. But the flesh is as infinitely destructive as it is cunning.

"Well?" my wife Betty says to me. "What do you intend to do about this now?"

"Fix it up right," I say and return to the machine, which is a delicate cubicle, man-sized, or woman-sized rather, about five feet six inches in height, three feet all around, just suitable for traveling if I wedge myself within. I turn the dials to *1933* and hastily go back in time.

"Fix it up right," I repeat to the bland inner surfaces of the machine. I have tried to furnish it in a somewhat homelike way with pictures of my family and two covers ripped from old pulp magazines, but it is difficult to dress up any cubicle five feet six inches in height and three feet all around. I ignore the pictures and instead absorb the sensations of traveling back in time, one year to three seconds, forty years, one hundred and twenty seconds or two minutes, that is to say. Travel in time is essentially uneventful; I think of it as being something like making love to my wife, Betty—an impenetrable surge of moments during which very little seems to happen until there is an eviction—but do not wish to be cruel to her. "I've got to solve this situation," I add.

What I have had in mind, of course, is to eliminate myself painlessly. Bills, obligations, job troubles (I have a very mundane civil-service position, but there has been reordering in the department and I am on the verge of losing my probationary status), marital woes, the general depression and fatigue of being a citizen of the twentieth century have overwhelmed me and what I want to do is to end it all in a way so final that it will have never happened at all. Killing one's grandfather is the classic means of doing this, according to the science-fiction stories I have read, but it does not seem to have worked. Therefore I will have to kill my father instead. Surely if I get rid of the old man—for whom I have always had a distant affection, I wish to emphasize that there is nothing personal in this and that parricide or grandparricide gives me no emotional satisfaction whatsoever—in 1933, four years before he met my mother, let alone married her, I will cancel out the fact of myself, to say nothing of my wife, Betty (she would have met and married someone else) and my twin daughter and son. Likewise the creditors and the ugly leakage that has begun to appear in the basement as the result of my experiments.

The dial comes to rest on *1933* with a *click!* and hastily I power down, reset the controls, and in a somewhat mole-like way emerge from my cubicle, giving the pulp-magazine covers and portraits of my family in repose a last affectionate glance. I am at Broadway and 87th Street forty years ago in what appears to be the late-afternoon rush hour, throngs of people passing me busily reading news of the bank closing, marvelous antique buses pouring fumes into the air and past my nostrils. No one appears to notice a blinking thirty-two-year-old man who has just emerged from a five-foot-six-inch cubicle, which cubicle instantly dwindles to the size of an apple and is picked up by this man to be inserted in his inner jacket pocket. As I recall, my father, before his marriage, lived with a friend in apartment 3B at 149 West 87th Street and hastily I set out in that direction. It is convenient that the machine has dropped me so close to the destination; calibration for space in what I like to call (pardon my vanity) Edgar's Device is still inexact and I could as well have been at the intersection of Broadway and Wall, watching some rich panic on the stock exchange. Time is my specialty, it seems; I am loose and sloppy on the space issue, but the fact that I have been able to calibrate so exactly gives me a little surge of feeling; surely this is a good omen and proves that I am on the right track. Now, all that I will have to do is to hope that my father is in, kill him promptly, and let events take their course.

I go into 149 West 87th Street unnoticed by passersby and two police who are inspecting a fire hydrant gone mad from the economic disorder of 1933 to hurl torrents of rusty water down the pastoral aspect of 87th Street of forty years ago, find my father's name listed in the vestibule and, pushing open the door—building access was easy in these times; the crime wave did not get really bad until after the war—sprint up the two flights to 3B, knock on the door once, and then, unbidden, walk in.

I find my father, much younger than I ever knew him, of course, standing in his undershirt by the window, looking out at the street and the accident of the fire hydrant. He turns toward me, his eyes blinking and full of light, and raises a hand in greeting. A merry man. I never knew him this way. He must have been quite a merry man, however, before he met my mother.

"Hello," he says, "how are you? I don't believe I know you, but that's perfectly all right. Maybe you're the man with the salt?"

He must be referring to some obscure forty-year-old grocery errand, but then again *salt* may have a peculiar local significance which escapes me. "No," I say in any event, "I'm not the man with the salt."

"Ah," he says, "that's a pity." He turns back toward the window. "If they don't seal that hydrant soon, New York's going to be underwater," he says, "and then I won't have to go to work tonight. Which, come to think of it, is all right with me."

As I recall, my father was a used-car salesman at this period of his life; a virginal used-car salesman, as a matter of fact and according to testimony, but then again, and as Thomas Wolfe once said, who can know his father's face? and this is not my concern at the present time. The time to have established a relationship with my father was in 1947 or thereabouts, certainly not in 1933, eight years before I was born or, properly speaking, even in seed form. "You're never going to work again," I say and, reaching into my suit pocket (not the pocket with the dwindled time-machine, the *other* pocket, the one with the .32 caliber Smith & Wesson), take out the pistol. "I'm going to kill you," I say to him matter-of-factly.

"That's ridiculous," he says, not turning from the window. "No one's going to kill me. This is 1933, it's modern times, and people just don't shoot strangers in their own apartments. People don't come off the street and kill strangers for no reason."

"You're not a stranger," I say. I feel a little pity for the old man, now so young and confused in his undershirt; it would have been nice if we had established some kind of relationship, I think, but then again we were never able to talk to one another (which is one of the reasons why I became neurotic and wound up in a mundane civil-service job, piddling around with time travel as a hobby instead of making a lot of money for myself) and this is no time to start. "I'm your son," I say nevertheless. "I've got to kill you."

"My son?" he says, turning, hands on hips. "I have no son and besides if I did he'd be a wee infant, not a big guy like yourself, about thirty-nine years of age, I'd say."

"I'm not thirty-nine," I say angrily, the gun shaking. Always, always the old man was able to get my goat. "I'm thirty-*two* and I'm unhappily married in a mundane civil-service job with bills way over my head and I've decided to end it all by getting rid of you. It's all your fault."

His eyes widen or perhaps in my excitement I think that they are widening when they are merely deepening. "You must be crazy," he says.

"I'm not crazy. I come from 1973, forty years from now. I was born in 1941, four years after you were married to a girl you won't even *meet* for four years, and frankly you were a lousy parent, but I don't even want to get *into* that area now. All I know is that if I kill you now you'll never meet the girl or get married and have me, and that means I never will have been born to be in this lousy mess. It's not your fault," I say, leveling the gun. "I mean, there's nothing personal in this. Even if you had been a *good* father I'd still want to kill you. But we were never able to have a good relationship, every time I tried to talk we got into these silly arguments about my shoes not being shined or why didn't I make something of myself in school, and I just can't get into all that stuff again. I'm sorry," I say and, concentrating hard, start to pull the trigger. It is really a very difficult and embarrassing thing, I have just discovered, to commit parricide. Grandparricide is easily possible—for one thing, I had never *met* my grandfather, who was dead years before I was born—but the father-son relationship is profound with, as they say, many Freudian overtones.

Thus, I am still concentrating on the effort of pulling the trigger and battling a deep sense of remorse when behind me there is a bang of the door and the two patrolmen whom I saw on the street enter the apartment purposefully. Skillfully they surround me, skillfully I am disarmed, skillfully I am manacled and placed in their custody. There is not even any time to reach for the apple-sized object in my left jacket pocket, much less to try and explain the situation to anyone. Before I quite know what has happened I am very much in the hands of the Depression police and being led gently enough down the stairs. "Don't worry about this one," one of the police calls upstairs to my astonished father, "we had reports that something like this might be going on in the neighborhood. You'll have to come down and give testimony later, maybe, but there's no reason for you to worry about anything like this." From two flights above, my father looks down at me open-mouthed and with some interest, but there is really very little that I could say to him—now more than ever we would have difficulty relating—and so I allow myself to pass from the building and into the street, where the Depression Era police walk me down to the corner, toward the precinct. It seems that in these times of apple-selling and bank holidays New York's finest do not have cars at their disposal, although then again they may be specially detailed foot patrolmen. The hydrant, I notice, is no longer gushing.

It must all have been a blind to make their presence on the prospective murder scene natural and acceptable and I realize then that all along I have been outsmarted and that probably they were waiting for me.

"You must have had advance knowledge," I say, being half-lofted in their strong arms, my little feet scuttling delicately on the gray but pleasant pavement of old New York, "someone must have told you that I was coming." Cunningly I try to reach an arm inside my jacket to get the time machine, but they are far more cunning than I, the hand is slapped away, another hand inserts itself and deftly removes the machine. The patrolman to my right looks at it with a delighted expression. "And there's the evidence," he says, "we've got him cold."

"You'll pay every bill you owe, buddy," the other policeman advises. "You'll work hard and you'll meet your debts and be responsible to your family. If there's one thing I can't stand," he says with a trace of disgust, "it's seeing a man trying to avoid his responsibilities."

"How did you know?" I ask pointlessly as we whisk toward a stoplight. "Who told you?"

"We got a tip."

"I know you got a tip," I say rather desperately, "but around here who would know? Who could possibly *know?*"

"Never mind," the policeman holding the little machine says, "we have our methods. And we have our sources of information. Anyway, I think that you'd know this informant very well. She certainly knows *you,* friend, and is she mad!"

"She?"

"Her name is Betty," the patrolman on my left says amiably enough, "and if I were you, which fortunately I am not, I'd *never* want to go home again, which unfortunately you will have to because we have too many mouths already to feed in 1933 and, whatever you think, it's better up the line."

"Betty," I say, "Betty." The conniving, rotten woman. And then a certain sense of absurdity overcomes me or maybe it is a flash of the divine and I look beyond the flat, high buildings of old New York to the sky of the Depression looming over us, and I laugh.

the empty field

morio kita

Translated by Kinya Tsuruta and Judith Merril*

Ground underfootrutcarved with trucktiretrails: where
heavy sculptured treads crisscrossed tired grass gives up:
piles of gravel, hillocks of sand: at the far end of the
field some children slowly moving silhouettes against great
concrete pipelengths glowing white in encroaching darkness at the far end of day—mudsmears on cheeks nearly
invisible halfopen mouths seen almost more by ear than
by eye—words more seen than heard—
  —murmurous sense as of the underwater conversation
of small fish—
  —*can't you stand still?*
  —*but! eaten up by gnats!*
  —*what gnats? no gnats here!*

Translator's note: Certain Japanese words have been used here
because they have no precise English equivalents: *Kokoro*
means both "heart" and "mind": either word alone is in-
sufficient. *Ojisan* is roughly a combination of mister, mac, sir,
uncle, dad, hey you, mate, pops, and another "sir" for good
measure. *Nani-ne* is just what it sounds like in English.

17

—*no?—listen*—
—*listening:* faint many-voiced buzzing—
—*sshhh—listen*—

Brittle silence: dimming light: truckserried surface like some castoff paperthin dry scaled skin: buzzing?
—*hear anything?*—
—silence, stop-action: vacant field like a deserted stage after the village play—descent of thick night's curtain not so much concluding-or-concealing as revealing new perceptions: whiteness comes to eye—
—at the foot of the hill a cluster of men's shirts flutter like wash forgotten on the line at night: and it begins again—
—*what if it really happens?*
—*maybe it's not true?*
—*don't care if it's true or not—if it was just a story we wouldn't be standing here and whispering*—
—*we could run over there—and yell—and make faces —and*—

Youngman also stands still as captive audience awash in airless-whispertide of senseless fish-communication pouring in through his perhaps-also-halfopen mouth—
—*but if it is true?*
—*then we really run: that way—like locusts!*
—*either way we run?—we run one way or the other, sure!—well sure we've been standing still too long already*—
Youngman moves a foot forward again: a step: conscious of movement of legs and of time gone by since he last walked toward no other purpose than the act itself—
—*what would it look like?*
—*like a snake?—or sea-squirt?—could be no shape at all*—
—*nothing like us anyhow!—how do you know?— dumb! if it was just like us they wouldn't be waiting there —we wouldn't be waiting here—have to keep still!—why would we worry about which way to run?*

—we could be sleeping like beansprouts in our beds—

Youngman starts past them:
—he too as a boy played in this vacant lot—but then
it was not barren like this: no trace of tiretracks: all green
—tall grasses growing-covering everywhere—
—all body-weight absorbed by thicknesses of grass
underfoot at every step—
—greenshoots moistcool and sensualclinging to foot
touch chest high in grass—grass invaded boy breathing
through grass—

Now—not a single treeleaf on the hill only marching
rows of raw new which-is-whose? company houses—and
the still yawning trench mouth of a bomb-shelter dug
during the war: cave-in-a-cave because the whole hill-
side then under bush canopy one green shadowdeep cavern:
magic expanse whose map was traced by busy beetles—
hoe-shaped, armored, others—along the ridged rough bark
of an old oak—
—soundless space where one drop of sap might startle
the poised shade-butterfly into flurried flight—tiny figure
swallowed by interleafed branchroof arch—
—and a child-explorer suddenly shrinks into small
helplessness drowned in the breathing of the towering
trees heart pounding tok!-tok!—
—*ojisan!*—chipmunk brazenbright boy's voice, dash-
ing the panic child memory—*ojisan: if you go over there
they'll just chase you away*—
—*chase me away?*
—*the way they look at you*—!
—*like a pregnant stray cat!*
—*maybe they don't chase grownups—maybe they'll let
him join—join the club*—?
—*join? club? what club?*—youngman asks.
—*people waiting up there*—boy's chin jerks toward
the hill—*they're waiting a long time for that thing to come
down*—
—*just waiting?*—asks the smallest boy.
—*well, they can't fly up! so they have to wait for it to*

*come down—they're trying to communicate with that
machine—some new kind of radio thing—and there was
a voice—*
    *—you heard the voice?—*that very small one asks.
    —well, they were saying—
    —it was different from our voice?
    —not like ours, like—like a praying mantis—
    —ojisan: you going over there?

No: youngman shakes his head and starts to walk,
leaving children behind, skirting sandpiles and pitfalls in
the dark, and the dim memories crowding into emptiness:
bare field: open clear spaces of a child's mind: clean
empty sponge sucking in from every side, every sign,
mixed promise and perception:
    *—red clay and concrete pipe become desert and moun-
tain—*for these boys, all children now and in the past, and
once himself: in dreams:
    *—diving in dew-drenched gravel piles where barren
trucktiretrails lead into magic forest heartlands—*youngman walks following such thoughts—

No! wallowing! in *their* fantasies because his own is
nothing but a dry and leafless hill, vacant place stripped
of wind-flowing grasses—where now in fact lead-legged
faltering kokoro unstrung he stumbles on ridged real
tiretracks chasing trace-memories of diaper-warmth and
the creased twilight of the womb:
Understood: the only certainty is entropy.

Ojisan: funny to hear himself called *ojisan:* not the
hilarity of the distorted image but instead the sudden
secret shock of recognition—nothing to do with years-of-
age, just *this-is-I-am-this:* true: skin and guts already dry-
ing out and hardened future clear to its farthest horizons—
endless detail-realities of everyday laid out through years
and years ahead glaringly visible across an empty space
where no trees offer cover.
    —that ojisan—
    —pretty sour—

—aah—grownups get like that—
—never want to talk except telling you what you're supposed to do!
—why do they get that way?
—shrug—no toys?—all tied up tight—
—like a fence gate with rusty wire—

Whispering voices follow and merge with gnat-buzzing fading behind: ahead the darkness thickens more and more: sight and sound dimmed, youngman walks: legs move but kokoro stands still stopped in the timeless place of children of all time—these, now, himself, short timeless time ago—burrowing sightless into thickets of dense undergrowth and tumbled pleasure where new worlds within expanding expose yet another burrow-grove entrance to yet another forestworld within—

Just so—just two years back, a student still, his own world turned upon the pivot of himself:
—drinking with a friend, *sake* on tonguetips tingling with vibrant words entangling and coalescing to give life and form to image and idea, whole cosmologies bursting from blind mysteries of youth's sensuality and mounting energy flowering into multitudinous shades and shapes of meaning—
—while all about the absolute brights and darks of the external world crowd in and out.

But I am in-and-out! seed-and-earth, body-and-cell, proton-and-atom—
—proton-self impelled by furious powers to explosion outward slowly slowed, ultimately contained by self-as-integral-atom:
—seedself unripe but fertile rooting in earth of the great-world-self: twisted and warped at present but with sureness of future time: interlinked, earth-seed-self-world in time together can mature.
Just so: so he believed: or had believed?

When?

Awareness faded in these few short days and months—
perhaps from the first time he put on a suit and tied his
tie to go to work—perhaps from that day life began to
merge with the inexorable click of the timeclock, life
counted out in number-counting till even the monotony is
hardly felt—

Busy-ness: time rushing by filled with the smell of office
heaters and screech of traffic brushing against dry skin:
body frozen so still finally even awareness of dryfreeze
evaporates—

—*you belong to the society?*
—*nnnhh?*

Two men in the darkness: one young man his own age,
large camera hanging from his shoulder, busy-brisk:

—*you don't belong to the group meeting here?*
—*no*—youngman shakes his head.

Cameraman nods curtly, steps back in darkness with
the other man—a sigh of irritation comes out from one
of them—

—*come on, let's get out of here!*
—*give it another thirty minutes—I broke my back
getting here!—let's wait and see if anything—*
—*you mean nothing, I tell you, nothing's going to
happen!—all we have to do is turn in the picture of these
nuts—*
—obviously, from some newspaper or magazine: what
for?

But their business seems less to the point than their
behavior—two people running like mad inside a space
the size of a slow snail's circuit—

—*no! I have no right to smugness like this—*

Youngman thinks:

—the world and all its people follow certain paths
planned or unplanned—

—*and I myself*—can it be, he is the only one untouched
by such vibrations?

Youngman wonders—alone inside this dried-and-pack-
aged existence, does nothing else remain?

If a mushroom cloud went up in front of him, even that would turn out to be empty—

Youngman expects nothing at all as calmly-surely as a child long back expected-looked to uncover hazy blue skies inside dark thickets of undergrowth: just so.

Sliding down the slope of the past he has come back to the same vacant field to find no trace of green growth left: only trucktracks cruelly dug into dirt.

But not quite so: in some far corners a few clumps of higher grass still stand and in one clump a dim bulking shape:

—*you there! watch out—a hole there!*

Youngman leans forward watchfully allowing himself to be steered in around the hole by the dry trickling voice:

—*here you are—grass here—*

Youngman takes the indicated seat:

—*nice cool evening—enjoying the air here?*

—*nani-ne—well, in a way—I gave my grandchild some fish-sausage and got told off for it, so—*

—like the fish-talk of the children, this old man's words make no more sense than the gnats' buzzing: but youngman bends a polite ear: dry-and-gentle voice as if the years have somehow husked it clean of both absurdity and agony of human busy-ness:

—*I fed the child a bit of fish-sausage, that's all—nothing wrong with it—fish-sausage is tender and nourishing—but my daughter-in-law doesn't like it: doesn't want me to feed the boy at all—she doesn't say anything of course, not a word out of her mouth: but it's clear enough: I understand—getting old, ears don't matter so much—learn to hear with other senses—*

Youngman nods absently—

His own life would soon certainly be consumed with just such daily non-events—devoured by trivia—like microscopic worms eating the body from inside till he was left an impotent old man preoccupied with grandchild and fish-sausage—

Youngman laughs politely:—*you live near here?*

—*live? no*—the husky voice seems to have no age now—*I come here sometimes—know these parts from very long ago—*

—*changed a lot, hasn't it?*

—*changed?—yes, of course, anything changes—*

—yet in the vacant lot there is no real change: built up with factory dormitories or something else in farther future still it would remain an empty place—

Lost in perspectives thus youngman continues to converse—

—*back in my childhood time grass grew all over here—*

—*hill had plenty of trees too—*

—*talk about that, there were plenty of people on the hill tonight—?*

—*yuh—they're still there: waiting for a saucer to come down.*

—*what did you say?*

—*saucer: what they call "sky-flying saucers"*—from the tone he could be talking about fishcakes still—*that's what they call them—*

Youngman peers into darkness at the old man's fuzzed face: remembers fragments of the children's murmurings —the journalists' exchange—something about a society to study flying saucers: people who say they meet space-visitors and exchange messages with them—all so ridiculous one does not even really want to laugh—

—*you don't believe in space-men?*

—*well-ll—I don't mind*—youngman, depressed, mumbles potato-mouthed—*suppose it's possible—*

—*yes*—the old man speaks very slowly, softly, seriously —*it is possible.*

No way to answer that—*those people over there— what are they—you know them?*

—*no: no—they're just waiting, that's all—saucer supposed to land over there somewhere—nah, getting old one's ears are bad but—*

—these people—what makes them think—do they know when—?

*—of course not—no: it could be any time:—*the statement is quiet and assured.

*—nothing to do with me—*youngman thinks and turns his eyes up to the few stars scattered in the cloud-hazed dark night sky—

—the stars used to have dignity and mystery—now soot and pollution dim their light and no one cares—*people have no time for stargazing anyhow—*

A single point of light shoots suddenly from mid-sky to cross the void: in spite of himself—

—aa-ahh!

*—a meteor—*says the old man at his side as if sharing his feelings.

Youngman laughs uneasily eyes still fixed on that corner of the sky: sitting so staring up in the same posture as those others on the hill, youngman's kokoro opens: consciousness—stubborn believers—tense fanatics—seedy ordinary people—baker, teacher, unemployed perhaps—staring up to the sky with desperate hope—all this vibrates through the night into youngman's kokoro overflowing:

—they must have something to believe in—and I too —simply believing is necessary—

Laugh it away: laughing empties the chest: into the chasm flows thick night air: long time youngman believes something not definite but certain things must be:

—the sky, eternally and infinitely deep: the stars, their ancient mystery regained: flight of white-silver darts of fire heating the night sky changing to crimson: hot red rain, raining—

—the gleaming transparent shape touches down on earth noiselessly: strange beings must appear—*like snakes? like sea-squirts? without shape?—*and everything will change: cities, towns, worn-out peace, even war: all values and all meanings—

—everything must change: and he himself—skin, bones,

spirit must renew themselves cell by cell step by step—
  —hungry for the first sign of change, youngman gazes at the sky, waiting, head back, breath caught—
  —*anything the matter?*
Dry cool old man's voice: dry ice dissolving the brief fantasy—belief more foolish than child's make-believe—
Bile burns in his throat: standing up woodenly young-man stammers:
  —*I'm—get on home—*

  oh you're going?—old man asks quietly—*looks like the kids are going too—*
True—over where the concrete pipes gleam white by night small shadows are detaching themselves one by one—
  —*everybody's going home, looks like*—the old man is looking at the hill now: nothing but darkness in that direction: but the old man nods as if concluding a performance and says in dismissal—
  —*well, good night!*

Youngman walks eyes fastened on the sky: thin scattered star-fragments disappear: fog already—or perhaps gathering clouds: dirt underfoot hard-dry and truck-dug tracks every now and then against his sole.
Alone in the empty place youngman quickens his steps following the children: still at some distance he feels echoes of the wash of fish-talk from them—
  —*I knew it—it didn't happen after all—*
  —*it couldn't really—*
  —*they just couldn't make contact, that's all.*
  —*hey! how come we didn't run?*
  —*nothing to run from, you dope!*
  —*running'll wear you down—like dried mushrooms!*
Youngman slows his pace:
  —*it just couldn't happen: nothing can happen.*

Child-shadows disappear—
Youngman's shadow gone—
The cluster at the hill-foot is dissolved.

Behind a clump of weeds, an old man sitting still—
Old man?—not quite that old man now.
Sitting still?—no wind but he is wavering somehow.
Something seems to be changing in the dark.

od

jack dann and george zebrowski

So they told me I'm in. Big deal. I'm in. But I did it myself, that's what they tell me.

They're all crazy, anyhow.

It's a small continuum, just about a mile across and stuck between two deterministic universes. It has a name —it could be Outer Dumbo, for all I know. So what? The two universes it's between are shaped like pears.

Anyway, OD never got to be fully real. No one really wanted to live like that. I mean, no one there really knows very much. For them knowing nothing—or as close to it as possible—is like knowing a lot. Really. One day I was arguing with a bunch of dudes, and one of them said I didn't know anything and—bang! I was there, gone, in the OD. The very place.

It's like a closet, this universe. There are lots of unknown words painted over all the rocks, like maybe someone had been in prison here a long time. There's this little stream which gurgles out of the rocks. And once in a while it rains, turning the ground into icky muck.

It really is a place to do nothing in. One of us—maybe me, even—had triggered the entrance, and the whole joint had opened up.

To me.

You see, it was your mind that got you in, nothing more.

All lies. That's not me. I have no clean-shaven face and pompadoured hair, and I don't speak slang and swear. I pull on my earlocks to feel my reality. I remember the Shema and the small shul with the rebbe named Feinberg who smoked Cuban cigars and liked a lot of women, including my Reisel, may she rest in peace.

That's real. I can still pray and taste my own saliva. This place is a hammock for my sins. God will punish. But why should I change into something worse than I already am?

I am becoming filth. My hair is greasy, sometimes. My earlocks disappear. The stream gurgles out of the rocks. And once in a while it rains, turning the ground into icky —into icy—into muck and filth.

They are returning. I must remain the same. I have a meeting with the taxman at four.

How the hell am I going to get out of here? I have appointments to keep, obligations to people I know. I have women to see. There are no women here. I need a secretary to take letters. Hired help is expensive, and very bad. If I'd had better hired help—well, I'd be saner. And I wouldn't be here now. Enough of this.

I've got to get out.

Still here. Something's wrong with the rubber band that links me to my world. It's not pulling me back. It got me here on a mindpull.

Lousy cheap rubber. Must have broke.

OD is starting to fill up. Guys who look like they're

waiting for a bus. Queuing up in line and looking up at the sky.

They won't talk to me. Maybe they have rubber in their heads?

So I pray. What else? It's raining and the stream is overflowing, rushing past into the filth beyond. Its foul water carries sticks and green bottles and probably important notes.

I have found certain things to be easier here. Since everything here is filth, there is nothing to do but pray for purity, a state man, and certainly I, cannot achieve. The stockmarket is real, my talis koton—which has also disappeared—my Feigle with her brown hair and pregnant stomach; they are all real.

So what? Here I can grow sideburns and swear. Part of me—such parts I cannot imagine—knows thoughts I could never imagine before. Jive. The slime beside the river is pomade for my hair. I perceive somehow—what matter how? —that I have left the taxman. It was very simple. He could not recognize me with my new face and attitude.

Bang. It's like a closet, this universe. Let my earlocks remain on the ghost in the synagogue. He rocks back and forth and thinks he's me.

I'm me. I'm alive!

OD has turned upside down. I've been walking on the ceiling for longer than I can remember. All the other dudes look like they've got beards on when I come near them. They have mouths in their foreheads, and poker-faced eyeballs.

I know what's going to happen. I really do.

OD is going to turn right side up. That's all.

There it goes.

Goodbye to all the beards and abiding eyes.

Ah, despair! Feet firmly on the ground again. The stream is swollen and flowing, somewhere in the night in front of me. There are no stars. It's restful, like a closet.

Oh, God, I am in the underworld. Alone, beyond repair,

beyond a good meal, beyond . . . beyond, beyond . . .

Words are disappearing from my mind. I feel them going. In the dull-glowing mornings I find words lying in the mud, thousands of words. All the words which have gone from my skull.

Soon my head will be empty. I will become the stones and the formless mud of OD, when the words for the RNA and DNA are emptied from my head.

The words are now a river, emptying from my soul. That's where all the words I saw when I got here came from.

They're all crazy with their misplaced eyes and toothless mouths. Sheol, the place without God, the entropy sink —how do I know such things?—that is sucking away at my mind. That's all there is now. This is real. *Gottenyu.*

I feel my thoughts being pulled away as I sit by the stream—fetid water—and let my toes curl in the slime. My prayers cannot rise here; they can only be sucked into nothingness. And that's what I deserve.

If I become hollow, slime will fill me up. Slime and strange words from that other person I'm becoming. I, too, will be Godless and misplaced. My teeth fall out. This is real. My talis, my phylacteries, my father's siddur— they're all made of air. Empty.

A terrible reality. These words and thoughts that fill me up are wrong. They're crazy.

A dybbuk's inside me, talking through my mouth (which is deformed and misplaced). He thinks that he's Satan and rules the slime. What can I do? I pray, anyway. God can't hear them, but I like the sound of the words.

Everything is crystal clear. I have a new mind! I know all the mysteries of this strange place. The mud rises up to praise me, because I can summon it with my words. A feast! A table set for my taste buds, cool ices for my food pipe!

The mud . . . rises into dark, vaguely human shapes which I invite to table with me. The mud eats with me.

We finish off the food.

There isn't enough. The shapes begin to gesture at me. There is hate in their mud arms. There is white mud in their mouths.

They rush me.

I lift my hand and swing at the first one. My hand goes into his heart, and I feel his mud heart beating, pumping red-brown mud.

In a few moments I am buried. I pulsate in the mud. I brood sullen under a starless sky. I hear the stream gurgling through me. My heart beats with the ebb and flow of the water which comes from nowhere.

My eyes are stones.

I open them.

An iron hammer shatters them.

I am blind.

Let it stay blind. Let it crawl inside me, scream, talk with its strange tongue with saliva that tastes like metal. It's raining again. My feet make sucking noises in the thick mud. I dance, flailing my arms about, singing songs that my father forgot.

If I slip and fall, taste the brown slime, what does it matter? I must be naked by now. The others are. But I'll dance alone to my own music and imagine them. They pray complacently in brick synagogues, eat fish and chase flies out of their filthy bedrooms so they can have sex. But the crawling things, hidden in the plaster, will watch. Good for them.

How long can I dance before I get tired? There is no air to breathe. My lungs are deflated balloons.

The sky is closer. I am more sullen. The closet continuum is shrinking. Its account is dry. They're closing it out. No funds. Not enough insanity . . .

Six hundred yards, five hundred yards, three hundred yards . . .

Two feet.

Six inches.

One micron.

Zilch.
Beyond zero.
I am waiting for the taxman to come back from lunch.

So they told me I'm in. Big deal. No more schizophrenic
episodes. I did it myself, that's what they tell me.
They're all crazy, anyhow.

amfortas

laurence m. janifer

date not relevant
Nur eine Waffe taugt:
Die Wunde schliesst der Speer
Nur, der sie schlug.

january 10, 2003
AP leased tapes, from Washington. The implant program has passed the "possible danger-point line" regarding side-effects, according to HEW Undersecretary Calvin Thomas in a statement released to newsmen this morning. "In the almost twenty-five years since the implant program was instituted," Mr. Thomas said, "no dangerous side-effects of the procedure have appeared. Implanting has been called the safest method of birth control, as it is certainly the surest: no properly implanted woman can possibly conceive a child during the effective lifetime of the implant, presently near forty years."

Pointing out that the implanting process can be reversed, Mr. Thomas went on: "Though many implanted women never have occasion to change their minds, such a change

34

is always in the cards: this, with the relative ease, the certainty, and, now, the proven risk-free nature of implants, makes them the optimum method of birth control developable. There is now no need whatever for a sexual encounter between man and woman to result in the birth of a child, unless that child is specifically wanted."

january 12, 2003

. . . having seeded additional lung tissue within soluble shielding, we began work matching the entire muscular, venous/arterial, and even skin structures of the donor segment to the left upper side of the patient. Matching was unexpectedly good, requiring no additional donor materials from the general bank. Blood flow began at once on cutoff of exterior support, and presented no unusual change in any respect. Clotting was controlled by the usual methods, the patient's skin having been laid back in a truncate-V flap at the sternal and scapular junctions, and the donor limb ligated without incident. Matching a single donor for a transplant of this extent may prove an additional risk, but no signs of risk were seen during operation. Entire area was shielded, pending intensive-care-unit shielding of entire patient to follow. The patient was directed to intensive care unit (pressure-locked) 5, on the housed table, attended as usual.

End notes for surgical record and report
Dr. Henry A. Sollen, M.D.
Dr. D. G. Haas, M.D., E.E.

february 22, 2003

Shirley, they tell me this is all going on tape through an induction mike, whatever that is. If I sound a little funny I have to talk without moving my mouth much, but don't worry about that, they tell me it's standard. I hope you're okay. I never felt that truck hit me, and the next thing I knew I was floating in this thing with my eyes taped shut, or glued shut, or anyhow something. It doesn't even *january 10, 2003*

INT CARE UNIT

PREPROGRAM 23327850	23327850	1	1	1	1	1

TEMP: SHIELD, CLOSED
32.222 C—90 F   TO RISE PRN TO AMBIENT EXT TEMP

TEMP: AMBIENT EXT
37 C—98.6 F

CONST SURVEY
EKG   EEG   SKIN   TEMP   PATTERN BPRESSURE BLOOD PH ELEC POTENTIAL AFFECTED AREA REM EXH PRODUCTS EXC PRODUCTS INDUCED SPEED NERVE IMPULSE PROPAGATION AFFECTED AREA GROSS MOTION AFFECTED AREA

AFFECTED AREA
L UPPER ARM   L LOWER ARM   L HAND   L DIGITS L THUMB L THORACIC STRUCTURE INC RIBS L LUNG PORTION L VENOUS AND ARTERIAL SYSTEM FASCIAE, MUSCLES, SKIN AS INDICATED

SPEC EQUIPMENT REQUIRED
CONST BATH INT SHIELD PRN   IV GLUCOSE R ARM   IV THALID6 R ARM IVs PRN R ARM

PRESSURE: INT SHIELD
1.1 ATMOS

PRESSURE: AMBIENT EXT
1.115 ATMOS

SPACE REQUIRED
INTENSIVE CARE PRESSURE LOCK 5

STAFF ON DUTY
MD   MD/EE   4   NURSING/INTERN STAFF   *AT ALL TIMES*

PATIENT
23327850   MORRIS BRADLEY D

OF
H A SOLLEN MD   D G HAAS MD/EE

PREPROGRAM ENDS
PREPROGRAM ENDS   PREPROGRAM ENDS   PREPROGRAM ENDS

hurt very much. The doctors tell me I'm not supposed to exert myself, and it would be very interesting to figure out a way to disobey them, floating here and attached the way I am to what must be the whole hospital, the way it feels. None of this stuff exactly hurts, but I can tell there is a lot of it there.

I can tell my left arm is there, too, and it doesn't feel new or anything like that at all. The doctors tell me the newness will come on me a little at a time, and a lot depends on the physical state of the donor, but more about him later. Right now it feels the way my left arm always felt. Not that I ever noticed it much.

The doctors are very impressed by how fast I'm getting better. One theory is that this time, with only a single donor to worry about, all the matching heals faster. This is the first time that's happened, for a whole arm and everything; usually, they tell me, it has to be built up a little here and a little there. Like a jigsaw puzzle?

I don't want to scare you with this stuff. It doesn't bother me, really. Once we'd signed on for the program I had a fair idea of what it might be like: we were either going to be donors or recipients, and I did a little reading.

But you were never scared by the details of anything, were you? I remember when we finally decided not to add to the population at all, just to get married in the synagogue to please your mother and live for ourselves after that—and we *will* get married just as soon as I get out, now. And you got your implant, is what I mean, and that was permanently that, and you started us both reading more about blood chemistry and hormone balance, all the adaptations that make it sure we won't have to have children. . . .

So I don't think this letter will bother you very much.

The doctors say the usual time on a thing like this is five months or more, but they think I might be out of here faster than that, healing so good. As soon as I get out of this "pressure environment" and into a normal intensive-care unit, anyhow, you can come and visit, and from there it's just one more move to a regular hospital bed, and then on home. I'm going to have to take it easy for a while, but you tell your mother she can start making wedding plans. After all, we've got time, haven't we? And when we do get married I'll be entirely okay—I mean, in bed and everything. Really okay.

It keeps me going, inside here when nobody's talking to me or anything, thinking that I'll be out and seeing you soon. And that when the doctors do okay me for full activity—bed and all; I don't think you're embarrassed reading this; bed and all—we can be married right away. And I'll be pushing them for that okay, and pushing hard. You better believe that.

This thing about the donor, by the way—I asked. They'll tell you a little, not very much, if you keep at it; and he was some sort of a drifter, not a regular signer for the program at all. But he looked healthy enough when they brought him in—I mean, he was *dead,* but he looked all right—and the kids who'd had their fun working him over hadn't really damaged too much. So he went right to the banks.

According to stuff in his pockets, he was a religious type, too. Not like your mother, or the way we are, the way most people are these days, but old-fashioned. One of the orthodox somethings, I suppose. And I guess God or Whatever took care of him one way, and me another.

A nurse told me he'd had a piece of old paper in one pocket with a line written on it. Really old: pen and ink, all hand done. *In this world, all life is a torment; and all life is sacred.* And if that's how he felt I guess he ended up on the right side of this donor-recipient agreement.

I know I did, anyhow. And soon, now . . .

june 15, 2006

DR. SOLLEN: Frankly, I'm no more surprised now than I was three years ago. It was a textbook job, the sort of thing one never expects; we had no trouble at all, and let me tell you *that's* enough for Dr. Haas, and me too, to

use up all the surprises we were saving for the next fifty
or sixty years.

1ST NEWS: And so, now, Bradley Morris can begin to
live an entirely normal life—the longest-surviving transplant case involving so large a body percentage.

DR. SOLLEN: Actually, we told him all restrictions were
off a few days ago. But I imagine he was still a bit cautious
—after all this time, of course, you know. Major grafting
of any sort is a shock to the system, as everyone knows:
the acclimatization, the relearning of nerve pathways . . .
but the graft is over three years old, and Mr. Morris is
forty: now he can begin, without fear, to live the normal
life of a normal forty-year-old man.

1ST NEWS: That includes, as our viewers know who
have seen the touching and archaic ceremony filmed
earlier today, a normal marital life.

DR. SOLLEN: Indeed. There was a celebration after the
wedding itself, you know—in fact, I left it to come down
for this interview. Oh, yes, he invited all of us . . . danced
at his wedding, in fact—so to speak, that is: fact being,
I *don't* dance. Never learned, couldn't say why.

1ST NEWS: And you feel that—that the strain will be
something his body can withstand?

DR. SOLLEN: No reason to suppose otherwise. By now,
he must be balanced quite completely; and, as I said, it
was a remarkable case. Everything simply—fitted together.
Entirely satisfactory; a great relief to us all, and a sign of
hope for the future. Needless deaths, needless injuries . . .
well, as the permanent-implant program reaches new
heights, and the population steadily reduces itself, there
will be *room,* room and to spare, for all those we can
bring back to full function. . . .

june 15/16, 2006

ESC OFFICER ANSWERING COMPLAINT: T. Sidden.

PRECINCT OR DEPT: 151 Precinct

NATURE OF COMPLAINT: Noise of fighting, apartment
overhead.

COMPLAINANT: Mrs. Bertha Wellesley.

ADDRESS: 1-151-6 Broome St., Apt. 6NN

IMMEDIATE PROCEDURE: On interviewing Mrs. Wellesley, I proceeded upstairs to apartment 7NN, which was
now entirely silent. On entrance with precinct-charged
passkey, I discovered the bodies of Mr. Bradley D. Morris,
tenant, and his wife (married that morning in a 3Vised
ceremony), Mrs. Shirley Ganz Morris, both subsequently
identified by sublandlords of building section. Mrs. Morris
had been stabbed once in the heart, Mr. Morris, once in
the throat. Mr. Morris was holding a large curved kitchen
knife in his left hand. The knife appeared capable of in-
flicting the wounds observed, though Mr. Morris, according to relatives, was right-handed.

SUBSEQUENT PROCEDURE: Detective squad and Homi-
cide NorthEast squad, called from phone in apartment
6NN, took immediate jurisdiction of case and prepared
all subsequent reports and papers.

NUMBER THIS REPORT: 1151-6-16-75

october 6, 2006

DISPOSITION OF COMPLAINT FORM: FINAL
NUMBER: 1151-6-16-75

DISPOSITION: Bodies identified by relatives. Grand jury
action brought against Bradley D. Morris, deceased: murder and suicide. No further action taken or contemplated.
Bodies released to Division Ten Hospital in accordance
with donor-recipient agreements made November 2002.
Deduction that knife had been used by left hand, due to
weapon having been found in left hand though Mr. Morris
was right-handed, and due also to autopsy report details
(see form 12 for this complaint), deemed of no significance.

date not relevant

The primary purpose of sexual activity is procreation.
Where this purpose is frustrated by deliberate consent or
action of either party, a sin has been committed.

date not relevant

The wages of sin is death.

january 1, 2003
DONOR: Available for use in whole or part at any time.
State of apparent continued preservation remarkable. No
known identity; entered Division Ten Hospital DOA,
gang attack. Pockets contained various papers, keys, no
money or valuables. Note actual brand across chest area.
This brand consists of Hebrew letters, forming the word
usually transliterated as *Lazarus*. Police official research
states that brand provides no clue to identity of donor.

date not relevant
One weapon only serves:
This wound will not be healed
Save by the spear that made it.

after king kong fell

philip josé farmer

The first half of the movie was grim and gray and somewhat tedious. Mr. Howller did not mind. That was, after
all, realism. Those times had been grim and gray. Moreover, behind the tediousness was the promise of something
vast and horrifying. The creeping pace and the measured
ritualistic movements of the actors gave intimations of
the workings of the gods. Unhurriedly, but with utmost
confidence, the gods were directing events toward the
climax.

Mr. Howller had felt that at the age of fifteen, and
he felt it now while watching the show on TV at the age
of fifty-five. Of course, when he first saw it in 1933, he
had known what was coming. Hadn't he lived through
some of the events only two years before that?

The old freighter, the *Wanderer*, was nosing blindly
through the fog toward the surflike roar of the natives'
drums. And then: the commercial. Mr. Howller rose and
stepped into the hall and called down the steps loudly
enough for Jill to hear him on the front porch. He thought,
commercials could be a blessing. They give us time to get
into the bathroom or the kitchen, or time to light up a

cigarette and decide about continuing to watch this show or go on to that show.

And why couldn't real life have its commercials?

Wouldn't it be something to be grateful for if reality stopped in mid-course while the Big Salesman made His pitch? The car about to smash into you, the bullet on its way to your brain, the first cancer cell about to break loose, the boss reaching for the phone to call you in so he can fire you, the spermatozoon about to be launched toward the ovum, the final insult about to be hurled at the once, and perhaps still, beloved, the final drink of alcohol which would rupture the abused blood vessel, the decision which would lead to the light that would surely fail?

If only you could step out while the commercial interrupted these, think about it, talk about it, and then, returning to the set, switch it to another channel.

But that one is having technical difficulties, and the one after that is a talk show whose guest is the archangel Gabriel himself and after some urging by the host he agrees to blow his trumpet, and . . .

Jill entered, sat down, and began to munch the cookies and drink the lemonade he had prepared for her. Jill was six and a half years old and beautiful, but then what granddaughter wasn't beautiful? Jill was also unhappy because she had just quarreled with her best friend, Amy, who had stalked off with threats never to see Jill again. Mr. Howller reminded her that this had happened before and that Amy always came back the next day, if not sooner. To take her mind off of Amy, Mr. Howller gave her a brief outline of what had happened in the movie. Jill listened without enthusiasm, but she became excited enough once the movie had resumed. And when Kong was feeling over the edge of the abyss for John Driscoll, played by Bruce Cabot, she got into her grandfather's lap. She gave a little scream and put her hands over her eyes when Kong carried Ann Redman into the jungle (Ann played by Fay Wray).

But by the time Kong lay dead on Fifth Avenue, she was rooting for him, as millions had before her. Mr.

Howller squeezed her and kissed her and said, "When your mother was about your age, I took her to see this. And when it was over, she was crying, too."

Jill sniffled and let him dry the tears with his handkerchief. When the Roadrunner cartoon came on, she got off his lap and went back to her cookie-munching. After a while she said, "Grandpa, the coyote falls off the cliff so far you can't even see him. When he hits, the whole earth shakes. But he always comes back, good as new. Why can he fall so far and not get hurt? Why couldn't King Kong fall and be just like new?"

Her grandparents and her mother had explained many times the distinction between a "live" and a "taped' show. It did not seem to make any difference how many times they explained. Somehow, in the years of watching TV, she had gotten the fixed idea that people in "live" shows actually suffered pain, sorrow, and death. The only shows she could endure seeing were those that her elders labeled as "taped." This worried Mr. Howller more than he admitted to his wife and daughter. Jill was a very bright child, but what if too many TV shows at too early an age had done her some irreparable harm? What if, a few years from now, she could easily see, and even define, the distinction between reality and unreality on the screen but deep down in her there was a child that still could not distinguish?

"You know that the Roadrunner is a series of pictures that move. People draw pictures, and people can do anything with pictures. So the Roadrunner is drawn again and again, and he's back in the next show with his wounds all healed and he's ready to make a jackass of himself again."

"A jackass? But he's a coyote."

"Now . . ."

Mr. Howller stopped. Jill was grinning.

"O.K., now you're pulling my leg."

"But is King Kong alive or is he taped?"

"Taped. Like the Disney I took you to see last week. *Bedknobs and Broomsticks.*"

"Then *King Kong* didn't happen?"

"Oh, yes, it really happened. But this is a movie they made about King Kong after what really happened was all over. So it's not exactly like it really was, and actors took the parts of Ann Redman and Carl Denham and all the others. Except King Kong himself. He was a toy model."

Jill was silent for a minute and then she said, "You mean, there really *was* a King Kong? How do you know, Grandpa?"

"Because I was there in New York when Kong went on his rampage. I was in the theater when he broke loose, and I was in the crowd that gathered around Kong's body after he fell off the Empire State Building. I was thirteen then, just seven years older than you are now. I was with my parents, and they were visiting my Aunt Thea. She was beautiful, and she had golden hair just like Fay Wray's —I mean, Ann Redman's. She'd married a very rich man, and they had a big apartment high up in the clouds. In the Empire State Building itself."

"High up in the clouds! That must've been fun, Grandpa!"

It would have been, he thought, if there had not been so much tension in that apartment. Uncle Nate and Aunt Thea should have been happy because they were so rich and lived in such a swell place. But they weren't. No one said anything to young Tim Howller, but he felt the suppressed anger, heard the bite of tone, and saw the tightening lips. His aunt and uncle were having trouble of some sort, and his parents were upset by it. But they all tried to pretend everything was as sweet as honey when he was around.

Young Howller had been eager to accept the pretense. He didn't like to think that anybody could be mad at his tall, blonde, and beautiful aunt. He was passionately in love with her; he ached for her in the daytime; at nights he had fantasies about her of which he was ashamed when he awoke. But not for long. She was a thousand times more desirable than Fay Wray or Claudette Colbert or Elissa Landi.

But that night, when they were all going to see the

première of *The Eighth Wonder of the World,* King Kong
himself, young Howller had managed to ignore whatever
it was that was bugging his elders. And even they seemed
to be having a good time. Uncle Nate, over his parents'
weak protests, had purchased orchestra seats for them.
These were twenty dollars apiece, big money in Depression days, enough to feed a family for a month. Everybody
got all dressed up, and Aunt Thea looked too beautiful to
be real. Young Howller was so excited that he thought his
heart was going to climb up and out through his throat.
For days the newspapers had been full of stories about
King Kong—speculations, rather, since Carl Denham
wasn't telling them much. And he, Tim Howller, would
be one of the lucky few to see the monster first.

Boy, wait until he got back to the kids in seventh
grade at Busiris, Illinois! Would their eyes ever pop when
he told them all about it!

But his happiness was too good to last. Aunt Thea
suddenly said she had a headache and couldn't possibly
go. Then she and Uncle Nate went into their bedroom,
and even in the front room, three rooms and a hallway
distant, young Tim could hear their voices. After a while
Uncle Nate, slamming doors behind him, came out. He
was red-faced and scowling, but he wasn't going to call
the party off. All four of them, very uncomfortable and
silent, rode in a taxi to the theater on Times Square. But
when they got inside, even Uncle Nate forgot the quarrel
or at least he seemed to. There was the big stage with its
towering silvery curtains and through the curtains came a
vibration of excitement and of delicious danger. And
even through the curtains the hot hairy ape-stink filled the
theater.

"Did King Kong get loose just like in the movie?" Jill
said.

Mr. Howller started. "What? Oh, yes, he sure did.
Just like in the movie."

"Were you scared, Grandpa? Did you run away like
everybody else?"

He hesitated. Jill's image of her grandfather had been
cast in a heroic mold. To her he was a giant of Her-

culean strength and perfect courage, her defender and champion. So far he had managed to live up to the image, mainly because the demands she made were not too much for him. In time she would see the cracks and the sawdust oozing out. But she was too young to disillusion now.

"No, I didn't run," he said. "I waited until the theater was cleared of the crowd."

This was true. The big man who'd been sitting in the seat before him had leaped up yelling as Kong began tearing the bars out of his cage, had whirled and jumped over the back of his seat, and his knee had hit young Howller on the jaw. And so young Howller had been stretched out senseless on the floor under the seats while the mob screamed and tore at each other and trampled the fallen.

Later he was glad that he had been knocked out. It gave him a good excuse for not keeping cool, for not acting heroically in the situation. He knew that if he had not been unconscious, he would have been as frenzied as the others, and he would have abandoned his parents, thinking only in his terror of his own salvation. Of course, his parents had deserted him, though they claimed that they had been swept away from him by the mob. This *could* be true; maybe his folks *had* actually tried to get to him. But he had not really thought they had, and for years he had looked down on them because of their flight. When he got older, he realized that he would have done the same thing, and he knew that his contempt for them was really a disguised contempt for himself.

He had awakened with a sore jaw and a headache. The police and the ambulance men were there and starting to take care of the hurt and to haul away the dead. He staggered past them out into the lobby and, not seeing his parents there, went outside. The sidewalks and the streets were plugged with thousands of men, women, and children, on foot and in cars, fleeing northward.

He had not known where Kong was. He should have been able to figure it out, since the frantic mob was leaving the midtown part of Manhattan. But he could think of only two things. Where were his parents? And was Aunt

Thea safe? And then he had a third thing to consider. He discovered that he had wet his pants. When he had seen the great ape burst loose, he had wet his pants.

Under the circumstances, he should have paid no attention to this. Certainly no one else did. But he was a very sensitive and shy boy of thirteen, and, for some reason, the need for getting dry underwear and trousers seemed even more important than finding his parents. In retrospect he would tell himself that he would have gone south anyway. But he knew deep down that if his pants had not been wet he might not have dared return to the Empire State Building.

It was impossible to buck the flow of the thousands moving like lava up Broadway. He went east on 43rd Street until he came to Fifth Avenue, where he started southward. There was a crowd to fight against here, too, but it was much smaller than that on Broadway. He was able to thread his way through it, though he often had to go out into the street and dodge the cars. These, fortunately, were not able to move faster than about three miles an hour.

"Many people got impatient because the cars wouldn't go faster," he told Jill, "and they just abandoned them and struck out on foot."

"Wasn't it noisy, Grandpa?"

"Noisy? I've never heard such noise. I think that everyone in Manhattan, except those hiding under their beds, was yelling or talking. And every driver in Manhattan was blowing his car's horn. And then there were the sirens of the fire trucks and police cars and ambulances. Yes, it was noisy."

Several times he tried to stop a fugitive so he could find out what was going on. But even when he did succeed in halting someone for a few seconds, he couldn't make himself heard. By then, as he found out later, the radio had broadcast the news. Kong had chased John Driscoll and Ann Redman out of the theater and across the street to their hotel. They had gone up to Driscoll's room, where they thought they were safe. But Kong had climbed up, using windows as ladder steps, reached into the room, knocked Driscoll out, grabbed Ann, and had then leaped away with her. He had headed, as Carl Denham figured he would, toward the tallest structure on the island. On King Kong's own island, he lived on the highest point, Skull Mountain, where he was truly monarch of all he surveyed. Here he would climb to the top of the Empire State Building, Manhattan's Skull Mountain.

Tim Howller had not known this, but he was able to infer that Kong had traveled down Fifth Avenue from 38th Street on. He passed a dozen cars with their tops flattened down by the ape's fist or turned over on their sides or tops. He saw three sheet-covered bodies on the sidewalks, and he overheard a policeman telling a reporter that Kong had climbed up several buildings on his way south and reached into windows and pulled people out and thrown them down onto the pavement.

"But you said King Kong was carrying Ann Redman in the crook of his arm, Grandpa," Jill said. "He only had one arm to climb with, Grandpa, so . . . so wouldn't he fall off the building when he reached in to grab those poor people?"

"A very shrewd observation, my little chickadee," Mr. Howller said, using the W. C. Fields voice that usually sent her into giggles. "But his arms were long enough for him to drape Ann Redman over the arm he used to hang on with while he reached in with the other. And to forestall your next question, even if you had not thought of it, he could turn over an automobile with only one hand."

"But . . . but why'd he take time out to do that if he wanted to get to the top of the Empire State Building?"

"I don't know why *people* often do the things they do," Mr. Howller said. "So how would I know why an *ape* does the things he does?"

When he was a block away from the Empire State, a plane crashed onto the middle of the avenue two blocks behind him and burned furiously. Tim Howller watched it for a few minutes, then he looked upward and saw the red and green lights of the five planes and the silvery bodies slipping in and out of the searchlights.

"Five airplanes, Grandpa? But the movie . . ."

"Yes, I know. The movie showed about fourteen or fifteen. But the book says that there were six to begin with, and the book is much more accurate. The movie also shows King Kong's last stand taking place in the daylight. But it didn't; it was still nighttime."

The Army Air Force plane must have been going at least 250 mph as it dived down toward the giant ape standing on the top of the observation tower. Kong had put Ann Redman by his feet so he could hang on to the tower with one hand and grab out with the other at the planes. One had come too close, and he had seized the left biplane structure and ripped it off. Given the energy of the plane, his hand should have been torn off, too, or at least he should have been pulled loose from his hold on the tower and gone down with the plane. But he hadn't let loose, and that told something of the enormous strength of that towering body. It also told something of the relative fragility of the biplane.

Young Howller had watched the efforts of the firemen to extinguish the fire and then he had turned back toward the Empire State Building. By then it was all over. All over for King Kong, anyway. It was, in after years, one of Mr. Howller's greatest regrets that he had not seen the monstrous dark body falling through the beams of the searchlights—blackness, then the flash of blackness through the whiteness of the highest beam, blackness, the flash through the next beam, blackness, the flash through the third beam, blackness, the flash through the lowest beam. Dot, dash, dot, dash, Mr. Howller was to think afterward. A code transmitted unconsciously by the great ape and received unconsciously by those who witnessed the fall. Or by those who would hear of it and think about it. Or was he going too far in conceiving this? Wasn't he always looking for codes? And, when he found them, unable to decipher them?

Since he had been thirteen, he had been trying to equate the great falls in man's myths and legends and to find some sort of intelligence in them. The fall of the tower of Babel, of Lucifer, of Vulcan, of Icarus, and, finally, of King

Kong. But he wasn't equal to the task; he didn't have the genius to perceive what the falls meant, he couldn't screen out the—to use an electronic term—the "noise." All he could come up with were folk adages. What goes up must come down. The bigger they are, the harder they fall.

"What'd you say, Grandpa?"

"I was thinking out loud, if you can call that thinking," Mr. Howller said.

Young Howller had been one of the first on the scene, and so he got a place in the front of the crowd. He had not completely forgotten his parents or Aunt Thea, but the danger was over, and he could not make himself leave to search for them. And he had even forgotten about his soaked pants. The body was only about thirty feet from him. It lay on its back on the sidewalk, just as in the movie. But the dead Kong did not look as big or as dignified as in the movie. He was spread out more like an apeskin rug than a body, and blood and bowels and their contents had splashed out around him.

After a while Carl Denham, the man responsible for capturing Kong and bringing him to New York, appeared. As in the movie, Denham spoke his classical lines by the body: "It was Beauty. As always, Beauty killed the Beast."

This was the most appropriately dramatic place for the lines to be spoken, of course, and the proper place to end the movie.

But the book had Denham speaking these lines as he leaned over the parapet of the observation tower to look down at Kong on the sidewalk. His only audience was a police sergeant.

Both the book and the movie were true. Or half true. Denham did speak those lines way up on the 102nd floor of the tower. But, showman that he was, he also spoke them when he got down to the sidewalk, where the newsmen could hear them.

Young Howller didn't hear Denham's remarks. He was too far away. Besides, at that moment he felt a tap on his shoulder and heard a man say, "Hey, kid, there's somebody trying to get your attention!"

Young Howller went into his mother's arms and wept

for at least a minute. His father reached past his mother and touched him briefly on the forehead, as if blessing him, and then gave his shoulder a squeeze. When he was able to talk, Tim Howller asked his mother what had happened to them. They, as near as they could remember, had been pushed out by the crowd, though they had fought to get to him, and had run up Broadway after they found themselves in the street because King Kong had appeared. They had managed to get back to the theater, had not been able to locate Tim, and had walked back to the Empire State Building.

"What happened to Uncle Nate?" Tim said.

Uncle Nate, his mother said, had caught up with them on Fifth Avenue and just now was trying to get past the police cordon into the building so he could check on Aunt Thea.

"She must be all right!" young Howller said. "The ape climbed up her side of the building, but she could easily get away from him, her apartment's so big!"

"Well, yes," his father had said. "But if she went to bed with her headache, she would've been right next to the window. But don't worry. If she'd been hurt, we'd know it. And maybe she wasn't even home."

Young Tim had asked him what he meant by that, but his father had only shrugged.

The three of them stood in the front line of the crowd, waiting for Uncle Nate to bring news of Aunt Thea, even though they weren't really worried about her, and waiting to see what happened to Kong. Mayor Jimmy Walker showed up and conferred with the officials. Then the governor himself, Franklin Delano Roosevelt, arrived with much noise of siren and motorcycle. A minute later a big black limousine with flashing red lights and a siren pulled up. Standing on the runningboard was a giant with bronze hair and strange-looking gold-flecked eyes. He jumped off the runningboard and strode up to the mayor, governor, and police commissioner and talked briefly with them. Tim Howller asked the man next to him what the giant's name was, but the man replied that he didn't know because he was from out of town also. The giant finished talking and strode up to the crowd, which opened for him as if it were the Red Sea and he were Moses, and he had no trouble at all getting through the police cordon. Tim then asked the man on the right of his parents if he knew the yellow-eyed giant's name. This man, tall and thin, was with a beautiful woman dressed up in an evening gown and a mink coat. He turned his head when Tim called to him and presented a hawklike face and eyes that burned so brightly that Tim wondered if he took dope. Those eyes also told him that here was a man who asked questions, not one who gave answers. Tim didn't repeat his question, and a moment later the man said, in a whispering voice that still carried a long distance, "Come on, Margo. I've work to do." And the two melted into the crowd.

Mr. Howller told Jill about the two men, and she said, "What about them, Grandpa?"

"I don't really know," he said. "Often I've wondered . . . Well, never mind. Whoever they were, they're irrelevant to what happened to King Kong. But I'll say one thing about New York—you sure see a lot of strange characters there."

Young Howller had expected that the mess would quickly be cleaned up. And it was true that the sanitation department had sent a big truck with a big crane and a number of men with hoses, scoop shovels, and brooms. But a dozen people at least stopped the cleanup almost before it began. Carl Denham wanted no one to touch the body except the taxidermists he had called in. If he couldn't exhibit a live Kong, he would exhibit a dead one. A colonel from Roosevelt Field claimed the body and, when asked why the Air Force wanted it, could not give an explanation. Rather, he refused to give one, and it was not until an hour later that a phone call from the White House forced him to reveal the real reason. A general wanted the skin for a trophy because Kong was the only ape ever shot down in aerial combat.

A lawyer for the owners of the Empire State Building appeared with a claim for possession of the body. His clients wanted reimbursement for the damage done to the building.

A representative of the transit system wanted Kong's body so it could be sold to help pay for the damage the ape had done to the Sixth Avenue Elevated.

The owner of the theater from which Kong had escaped arrived with his lawyer and announced he intended to sue Denham for an amount which would cover the sums he would have to pay to those who were inevitably going to sue him.

The police ordered the body seized as evidence in the trial for involuntary manslaughter and criminal negligence in which Denham and the theater owner would be defendants in due process.

The manslaughter charges were later dropped, but Denham did serve a year before being paroled. On being released, he was killed by a religious fanatic, a native brought back by the second expedition to Kong's island. He was, in fact, the witch doctor. He had murdered Denham because Denham had abducted and slain his god, Kong.

His Majesty's New York consul showed up with papers which proved that Kong's island was in British waters. Therefore, Denham had no right to anything removed from the island without permission of His Majesty's government.

Denham was in a lot of trouble. But the worst blow of all was to come next day. He would be handed notification that he was being sued by Ann Redman. She wanted compensation to the tune of ten million dollars for various physical indignities and injuries suffered during her two abductions by the ape, plus the mental anguish these had caused her. Unfortunately for her, Denham went to prison without a penny in his pocket, and she dropped the suit. Thus, the public never found out exactly what the "physical indignities and injuries" were, but this did not keep it from making many speculations. Ann Redman also sued John Driscoll, though for a different reason. She claimed breach of promise. Driscoll, interviewed by newsmen, made his famous remark that she should have been suing

Kong, not him. This convinced most of the public that what it had suspected had indeed happened. Just how it could have been done was difficult to explain, but the public had never lacked wiseacres who would not only attempt the difficult but would not draw back even at the impossible.

Actually, Mr. Howller thought, the deed was not beyond possibility. Take an adult male gorilla who stood six feet high and weighed 350 pounds. According to Swiss zoo director Ernst Lang, he would have a full erection only two inches long. How did Professor Lang know this? Did he enter the cage during a mating and measure the phallus? Not very likely. Even the timid and amiable gorilla would scarcely submit to this type of handling in that kind of situation. Never mind. Professor Lang said it was so, and so it must be. Perhaps he used a telescope with gradations across the lens like those on a submarine's periscope. In any event, until someone entered the cage and slapped down a ruler during the action, Professor Lang's word would have to be taken as the last word.

By mathematical extrapolation, using the square-cube law, a gorilla twenty feet tall would have an erect penis about twenty-one inches long. What the diameter would be was another guess and perhaps a vital one, for Ann Redman anyway. Whatever anyone else thought about the possibility, Kong must have decided that he would never know unless he tried. Just how well he succeeded, only he and his victim knew, since the attempt would have taken place before Driscoll and Denham got to the observation tower and before the searchlight beams centered on their target.

But Ann Redman must have told her lover, John Driscoll, the truth, and he turned out not to be such a strong man after all.

"What're you thinking about, Grandpa?"

Mr. Howller looked at the screen. The Roadrunner had been succeeded by the Pink Panther, who was enduring as much pain and violence as the poor old coyote.

"Nothing," he said. "I'm just watching the Pink Panther with you."

"But you didn't say what happened to King Kong," she said.

"Oh," he said, "we stood around until dawn, and then the big shots finally came to some sort of agreement. The body just couldn't be left there much longer, if for no other reason than that it was blocking traffic. Blocking traffic meant that business would be held up. And lots of people would lose lots of money. And so Kong's body was taken away by the Police Department, though it used the Sanitation Department's crane, and it was kept in an icehouse until its ownership could be thrashed out."

"Poor Kong."

"No," he said, "not poor Kong. He was dead and out of it."

"He went to heaven?"

"As much as anybody," Mr. Howller said.

"But he killed a lot of people, and he carried off that nice girl. Wasn't he bad?"

"No, he wasn't bad. He was an animal, and he didn't know the difference between good and evil. Anyway, even if he'd been human, he would've been doing what any human would have done."

"What do you mean, Grandpa?"

"Well, if you were captured by people only a foot tall and carried off to a far place and put in a cage, wouldn't you try to escape? And if these people tried to put you back in, or got so scared that they tried to kill you right now, wouldn't you step on them?"

"Sure, I'd step on them, Grandpa."

"You'd be justified, too. And King Kong was justified. He was only acting according to the dictates of his instincts."

"What?"

"He was an animal, and so he can't be blamed, no matter what he did. He wasn't evil. It was what happened around Kong that was evil."

"What do you mean?" Jill said.

"He brought out the bad and the good in the people."

But mostly bad, he thought, and he encouraged Jill to forget about Kong and concentrate on the Pink Panther.

And as he looked at the screen, he saw it through tears. Even after forty-two years, he thought, tears. This was what the fall of Kong had meant to him.

The crane had hooked the corpse and lifted it up. And there were two flattened-out bodies under Kong; he must have dropped them onto the sidewalk on his way up and then fallen on them from the tower. But how explain the nakedness of the corpses of the man and the woman?

The hair of the woman was long and, in a small area not covered by blood, yellow. And part of her face was recognizable.

Young Tim had not known until then that Uncle Nate had returned from looking for Aunt Thea. Uncle Nate gave a long wailing cry that sounded as if he, too, were falling from the top of the Empire State Building.

A second later young Tim Howller was wailing. But where Uncle Nate's was the cry of betrayal, and perhaps of revenge satisfied, Tim's was both of betrayal and of grief for the death of one he had passionately loved with a thirteen-year-old's love, for one whom the thirteen-year-old in him still loved.

"Grandpa, are there any more King Kongs?"

"No," Mr. Howller said. To say yes would force him to try to explain something that she could not understand. When she got older, she would know that every dawn saw the death of the old Kong and the birth of the new.

symposium

r. a. lafferty

"Perversity," cried ancient Swift,
"Of lifeless things," and cursed a skewer.
But some of them, with lilt and lift,
Were fuller up with life than you are.

Be there a jug devoid of juice?
A stick or stone with no life in it?
A shoe that has no sense of use?
Then name us such. Begin, begin it!

The wisdom of old furniture,
The panniers' passioned cerebration . . .
"They cannot be!" (But are you sure?)
. . . The Artifacts' cool speculation . . .

As reft of life as children's blocks,
The Things arise to balk and bait us.
Be it a chance such ricks and rocks,
Inanimate, could animate us?

I'M INANIMATE, YOU'RE INANIMATE—*Virgo Haedus*

The world begins, not necessarily for the first time.

Not with a bang, but a tumble. In the beginning was noise. A cataract of worlds or entities rolling and cascading in fearful clatter. The cosmic atom, the world-box, has disgorged. Here is bursting galactic expansion into free area. Avalanche of noise and bright color. Not chaos, but thunderous exodus; and every particle bearing its own thunder sign. This is beginning, this is happening! Let no least part of it ever forget the primordial tumble that is the beginning!

Then, the stable state—and memory. The first thought ever thought anywhere, anywhen: *It's as though I've been here before.*

The senses clear. There are persons present, high persons who can only be designated in code.

"Have I missed anything?" Kay spoke, for speech is always simultaneous with consciousness. "It seems I have just wakened. Is this the way the world begins?"

"Yes, I believe this is the way the universe begins every time," Eff muttered, "with entities waking to consciousness and conversing with their mature peers. At every world-beginning, the persons are born adult and intelligent. That business of being born puling and helpless is a late accretion, and there is no evidence that it is anything more than a fable or a fall."

"I am not alone?" Gee wondered aloud. "There are others and they discuss? Well, if we've got to have conversation, let's agree to keep it inside the frame. Oh, hello, Zee!"

"My name is Zed, for so it is called in the old country. Let's keep the frame moving, Gee, and anything we wish can be inside it. Look at anything through a frame, and it's a striking picture. There may be other frames, but we are limited to our own: space, time, motion, mass, and the vivifying principle, known to us through consciousness on its several levels, by means of the senses and parasenses, and aided by less than a dozen styles of thought. It's limited, but it's all we seem to have."

"And, Zed," said O doubtfully, "every one of those elements is shaky. We are unable to separate space from one of its elements—shape. We do not know whether the particular distortion we live in is one of shape or of space. For instance, with us, the relation of the ring to the tendon of a circle is three and a continuing decimal to one. But we know from Scripture, and also from the geometry of Jordman, that in undistorted space or shape the relation would be exactly three to one. Now, if we were in such an undistorted space or shape, might we not think undistorted thoughts? It is certain that we would think in a different manner and that every object of our thoughts would differ from the present. We would not have the same grammar or conventions."

"There is no undistorted space, O," Wye said solidly. "Distortion is a necessary element. If I be not distorted, then I be not at all. The shape of space depends on the amount of matter in the universe. Matter is the distortion, but no matter is nothing. The amount of matter posits its own mathematics. There cannot be theoretical mathematics, only the mathematics of an actual universe. But, should the mass of the universe increase by only an ounce (Nictitating nebulas!—that's a little too slight), should it increase by no more than a thousand galaxies, then every mathematical property would change. The ratio of the ring to the tendon of a circle might then become three and a half, or five, or nine, or one. There might then be thirteen whole numbers between one and ten.

"For my part, I believe that we *do* live in a universe of changing mass, and that every property changes with it. Do you know why nobody discovered certain simple relationships before Pythagoras did so? It was because they had only just then become true relationships. Do you know why nobody discovered the three laws of motion before Newton discovered them? And why Newton did not discover them before he did? Because—*they had not been true the day before*."

"But if the mass of the universe should be constant—" O interposed.

"No, no, forget it!" Wye bade him. "That raises more

difficulties than it solves. The neatest universe, which I believe to be the present and true one, has time as a constant, and everything else as a variable. This was hinted at by Aristotle and developed more fully by Aloysius Shiplap. Its implications (which include ourselves) are tremendous."

"You blockhead!" Zed exploded. "That constant-time universe, by definition, *must always have been thirteen billion years old*. And it cannot age by one more second without annihilating itself."

"Yes. Is it not a beautiful concept?" Wye beamed.

"Even less than of these things do we know about the vivifying principle," You cut in. "One person has said, in apparent contradiction to his senses, that nothing can exist without it. But his fellow contradicted him. 'Look at that rock,' he said. 'It exists, and it is dead matter. You are answered.' But was he answered rightly?

"We know the shell of our own world to a depth of no more than fifty thousand meters. But every rock, every piece of that known mantle, *has been* living matter. We cleared away the doubt about the main bulk of it fifty years ago. There is the possibility, if the fragments should be sufficiently analyzed, that every particle of the universe was first living matter before it was anything else. Life and matter may have been simultaneous and identical. Then the question, Whether life can arise from lifeless matter, becomes inverted. The question becomes: Can matter arise from anything except life? We should not ask: How did life appear? but: How did death appear? I believe death is the illusion. If any particle of matter should ever die, it would immediately disappear to every sense and meaning. It's all alive. The very rocks (I don't see any rocks right now, but I know of them intuitively) could get up and walk away if they wished."

"But the inverted form of the question hasn't been accepted by anyone except yourself, You," En cut in, "and I've heard that it's mighty lonesome to be a minority of one. The rest of us will still ask: How did life appear, by accident or by design? The man of the house here (how do I know about a man or a house or an exocosmos at all?) has a small electrical appliance there on the sideboard; it has an electric motor in it. I ask you, You: How did the first electric motor appear, by accident or by design?

"It's a simple little four-pole thing. Nothing is needed but a small amount of copper, iron, and insulating material—all of them things found in nature. We assume that the first motor was very simple, but could it have originated by accident in a primordial swamp, workable and working? We must assume a power source—accidental, of course—and some random sort of transmission lines. There aren't, when you strip the unessentials away, more than a few hundred items that have to fall together in the right pattern to achieve it. But I maintain that accident could not have accomplished it.

"And I also maintain that the most simple living cell is a billion to a billion powers times as intricate as the most sophisticated motor. It's improbable that an electrical motor could have appeared by accident, complete with name plate and with greasing instructions printed on an attached tag. And the difference in probability is staggering. Boys have made motors. Who has made a cell?"

"Ah, En, permit me to exercise my talent for fiction and for irony." Ex essayed it. "I posit a primordial swamp in which is found a long glob of natural copper fused by lightning. In an accidental manner the copper has become looped three times around another glob of volcanic iron. I posit natural lodestone somehow to form a field. I posit proto-mica wedging itself into position as insulator, and a shaft of accidental design, and good honest mud as a bearing surface."

"But several of your items were formed during organic periods, Ex," En objected. "They would not be found in a *truly primordial* swamp."

"No matter, En, we'd find something else to serve as well. Close by, I posit a stagnant pool a little different from the other pools. Chance metallic solutions have given it polarity potential in its acid constituent. It hasn't a brand name on it, but it is a battery. (In the beginning, God made d.c., and the alternator was not as yet.) I posit conductors of some sort, I forget just what, and several hundred other details that will come easy to a swamp with all the time in the world. It is ready! It happens! And I swear by all primordial things that it is witnessed!

"For I also posit two rocks rubbing together in a high wind. 'It turns, it turns!' is the sound the rocks make as they rub together. 'Tell all the boys that it turns.' "

"You are trapped by your own narrowness, Ex," said Eye. "You are considering whether a thing might be so or might not be so, as if there were no other alternatives. Believe me, the multiplex alternator came first. Let us consider what is beyond categories. You see a circle, a form: but what if we go beyond the idea of form? You think of a number: but what if we are in a country where there can be no idea of number, where neither unity nor diversity has any meaning, where neither being nor non-being can be conceived of?

"You think of space. What if there are a hundred alternatives to space, and I do *not* mean a hundred alternative kinds of space. What if there are a thousand other things in the category with living and dying? We operate according to one sort of grammar and we view the world by its syntax. Let us view it from the no-framework of no-grammar. I could go on with it, but the terminology becomes insufferably cute. *What was that jolt?* It's the noise the world always makes just before it ends. How do I know that, since I've never seen a world end before? Megagalactic memory, I suppose. After all, we're supposed to think of these things. We are seminal contrivances."

"How do you know that we're seminal contrivances?" Are asked, puzzled.

"It says so on the box," Ex told him.

"We work with what we have," said Are. "Let the inconceivables bury their own dead. I believe that every point is the center, even though in your land, Eye, the idea of a center disappears. I stand and say that I am the medium of all things, that there are as many things smaller than me as there are larger. But the meanest parasite in a sub-atomic civilization may say the same thing, and so may the shambling oaf whose outline is made up of clustered galaxies. But I ask you: Does this go on forever, or is it circular? The people (or is it the robots?) say that people and robots alternate in cycles. People make robots. Then, after a million years, the robots make people again. Then the robots die out and the people reign alone. After a decent interval, the people make robots again. And the people die once more. There have been many of these cycles. We ourselves are neither people nor robots, though I do not at the moment remember just what we are.

"But as to size, is it re-entrant like space and time? Will the smallest of particles, a million scales descended, look through the ultimate microscope and see the nine thousand billion greater galaxies as a mere hint of light at the lowest limit of vision? And if space and time and size be all re-entrant, may not categories be so also? Perhaps the no-concepts of Eye do not go on forever (though they easily might go beyond the concept of ever). May they not return, each one eating his ultimate grandfathers like a handful of peanuts, and discover that they have become concepts once more? The only theory of cosmology that satisfies is that every star or body should become in sequence every other star or body. The only theory of reincarnation that satisfies is that every person should become in sequence every other person. Looking around me, I don't think I'll like it."

"I feel it too now, Eye," said Pea. "It's the end of the world all right, the *synteleia,* the kid with the box, the latter days when our philosophy fails us. One thing happened to us, the clattering tumble. We appeared. They can't take that away from us. If there should come a second high happening, then we are doubly blessed. Well, they've never let us finish a talk yet, but we'll talk while we live. What do you think: Is it all a circle eating itself? And are all of us but shadows in the mind of each of us. If I have no existence except that Ell has dreamed me, and he has no existence outside of the mind of Ess, and if so around the circle of the twenty-six of us—"

"The twenty-seven of us!" Thorn roared thunderously.

"I am here! And you are all in my mind, not I in yours. The proof is that you forget me in your count and I do not fit into the box. I am the only one with true consciousness, and that brings us to an interesting point. Did consciousness come to us by physical analogy? How is the double thing (consciousness, that which regards itself) born in a single mind? Is it not by analogy with the double orifices that lead into that mind? We know that the duostomata have the most vivid consciousness of all creatures. And the only one-eyed intelligent race yet discovered, the Yekyaka, has missed consciousness completely. Hey, somebody break out the cigars and brandy if we're going to talk! Question: Are cigars and brandy intuitive concepts?"

"It is true that you view us from the outside, Thorn, and for the simple reason that you are not here," said Tea. "Ah, I do love a gracious snifter and a good cigar. I wonder what the poor people are doing tonight."

"The non-elites?" Thorn asked. "Why, Vee and Cue and Jay and their fellows are spelling little riddles over toward the edge of the table there."

"But you are not here, Thorn," Tea insisted. "You went out of existence so long ago that it is only by accident that we remember your name. You are the shaggy fringes sticking out from the framework. You belong to the spooks, the sports, the meteorological monstrosities. Dammit, Thorn, you just don't fit in! To us you are awkward, and awkwardness is the sin that will not be forgiven in this world or the next. *Whoops! Hold on to your hats, boys!* I hear those end-of-the-world noises too!"

"So I am awkward, a spook, am I, Tea?" Thorn demanded. "Tea, you can't get rid of the awkward. It does not really dispose of a thing to call it Fortean. I offend because I'm an old-timer who remembers when everything was larger. I was talking to a crony recently. 'They don't make planets the way they used to,' he said, 'they don't make stars and stuff as well. Time gets tired, and light, and matter. Everything shrinks, but the measuring stick shrinks also, so nobody notices. I tell you, I remember light that was light,' he said, 'I remember molecules of acetophenone-ketone that were as big as horses, and some mere atoms were as big as the house cats now. The light then would shatter a steel plate of today, the minutes were as millennia, the pounds each weighed a million tons. It was grander and shaggier in the old days.' My crony was right, but so few of us remember those times. Hey, it's coming for you guys now! There's an advantage to not fitting in. I don't have to go."

"It's upon us!" cried Ell. "We've talked for our thousand years, and the world collapses! Time is foreshortened! Our brains melt like wax!"

CHILD (sex unknown; the way they dress them now, it's hard to tell): "Blocks! Jump! Jump in the box if you want to get out again tomorrow. It's time to get back in the box."

THE BLOCKS: "Woe, woe, woe! It's the *synteleia,* the kid with the box, the final happening that voids all happenings."

CHILD: "All in but one! Jump, jump in! Oh, no, no, you're the one that doesn't belong. I don't know where you always come from. Get out of here. You're crazy."

MOTHER (or FATHER—the way they dress them now, it's hard to tell): "Ah, you have been playing with the alphabetical blocks, Iracema. These are good ones. Chatter-blocks in the Chatter-box, it says. They have little coils inside them and they react to each other. Sometimes they seem to talk and think. They are seminal blocks. That's what the toy salesman said."

PARENT (the other one, the one with the longer hair): "Educational toys are good."

swords of ifthan

james sutherland

For Alvin Moffet, the quintessence of Life As It Should Be was contained within a row of leather-bound volumes in the library's rare-book room. Alvin worked one floor below, at the reference desk, but passed his spare moments upstairs savoring *Le Morte d'Arthur*, perhaps, or *Orlando Furioso*. When an influx of students kept him at the desk—during final-examination weeks, usually—he made do with a cheap edition of *The Once and Future King* and his own glowing dreams. And though he admired the former's vision, in his heart Alvin felt the latter remained truest to the spirit of the old classics.

One noontime he came upon a nacreous sphere floating alongside *The Song of Roland*.

"Alvin Moffet?" the sphere inquired briskly. "Alvin Bergen Moffet?"

Distracted, Alvin nodded vaguely.

The sphere bobbled. "Excellent! I have journeyed far to meet with you."

At this point Alvin fully perceived he was being addressed by an altogether strange entity, flinched, and cried in confusion: "Whaahoowhere?"

Fortunately the sphere seemed to understand, and replied that it was no less than the Guardian of Continua, coming to seek Alvin's assistance in a matter of desperate urgency.

"Whatever can I do?"

"Aid the fair world of Ifthan, which presently lies in much danger." Alvin had never heard of Ifthan, so the Guardian added in hurried tones: "I will construct a visual simulacrum of Ifthan, adjusted to your senses. Observe, then, and quick!"

Around Alvin the somehow familiar landscape of Ifthan took form. Here were green glades and forests; there were softly rolling meadows; and beyond, a gleaming castle. A lone knight ventured from the raised portcullis and warily rode toward a monstrous dragonlike creature that was laying the countryside to waste and ruin. From a high revetment a raven-haired woman of surpassing beauty called passionate encouragement to her hero as he spurred his mount near the dragon. A sword flashed under the golden sun. . . . The scene faded mistily.

"As your eyes beheld," continued the sphere, "Ifthan is besieged by those loathly invaders. Our champions are powerless to resist the ever advancing tide. Only a valiant outsider can be an equal to the unnatural foe."

"You want *me?*"

"Assuredly." The sphere seemed to read Alvin's thoughts by concluding: "Fear not; the Earthly physique that you deem inadequate will be suitably rectified if you choose to accompany me. Now, will you accept this awesome challenge?"

It's everything I've ever read about, dreamed about, hoped for, Alvin thought, scarcely daring to breathe. He decided.

"Where do I sign?"

"Your word is proof enough of intent, Alvin Moffet!"

Abruptly the Continuum slewed wildly, then Alvin found himself standing in the selfsame meadow beside the castle he had glimpsed. The air was wonderfully fresh and hearty, and Alvin let out a happy yell that quite suddenly ended as he noticed he had just exhaled orange flames. Looking down in mounting horror, he discovered that his skin had turned a scaly magenta, his fingers had dwindled to jagged claws, and his legs were grotesque stumps.

"This isn't what I'd expected," Alvin said angrily, lashing his heavy spiked tail about like a bullwhip.

"Careful with that thing," the sphere said anxiously. "Wait for the signal."

A crowd was beginning to gather along the revetment, screaming at Alvin and making gestures. When a plumed knight of heroic proportions thundered out the castle gateway, they shouted in ecstasy. The knight pointed his lance at Alvin and the crowd whooped with delirious anticipation.

Made wretched by the turn of events, Alvin wanted to weep. But reptiles have no tear ducts: all he could choke out was a reproachful, "I . . . I don't know what to think of this, or of you!"

"Think of me as your manager. Now lissen good, kid," the sphere told him in a hoarse and sweaty-sounding voice. "When the gong sounds, I want you to really get in there and *fight!*"

beast in view

miriam allen de ford

We Earth-descended colonists on Alpha Centauri IV—
which we call Albia—aren't much given to competitive
sports or to physical competition of any kind: it's too
hard to breathe in this thin air. So perforce we've gone in
for Intellect and Art. Culture: we're undoubtedly the most
cultured Earth colony in the galaxy.

All but Johnny Newson. Johnny was a throwback—
what our ancestors used to call motor-minded. He'd have
been wonderful in a bullring or a machine shop or on a
battlefield. But, naturally, he was a misfit among us.

Most of us Albians are of English descent, with a few
stemming from Old France and a sprinkling from Old
Holland. (Oh, and a few also from Normerica, all pos-
terity of some primitive Tribe of Wasp, whose totem was
a stinging insert.) Johnny was mostly English too, but I
swear he must have had a touch of Apache from somewhere.

Because, besides everything else, we are strictly pacific,
whereas Johnny was always spoiling for a fight: a fight
that never came off, since nobody else felt the same way,

so it curdled inside him and made him sour.

You notice I speak of him in the past tense. No more Johnny. Let me tell you what happened.

Johnny wanted to fight, but there was nobody for him to fight with. So he rediscovered hunting; and being motor-minded as well, he reinvented the bow and arrow. All highly illegal, of course; and he kept it secret as long as he could.

There is very little wildlife on Albia, and what there is is harmless and protected.

Johnny came back from the woods dragging the carcass of a xenophere. The xenophere is a woolly beast something like an enormously overgrown sheep—herbivorous, like all our animals. It can run pretty fast, so we've tried to ride it, but though it's docile it is too stupid to follow directions. This specimen must have just stood still for Johnny Newson to slaughter it.

That was the year I was elected Chief Guardian of our settlement. It was up to me to do something about Johnny.

Among the treasures in our library is an old book—not a microfilm, a real book made of paper, apparently brought here by one of the Founding Parents. The title and half the author's name are torn off; it's by somebody named something starting with "Gil." In it (it seems to be some kind of drama) there is a song about making the punishment fit the crime.

Well, I couldn't stand Johnny up and shoot him with his bow and arrow.

And what was I supposed to do with the dead xeno-phere? We eat mostly organic vegetables and fruit and recycled synthetic meat—certainly not this native animal.

I had Johnny brought in. He wouldn't sit down, just stood by my desk and glared at me. Thinking of that song, I said, "First thing, Johnny, you've got to dig a big hole and bury that creature before it begins to smell."

He looked aggrieved. I swear, he was *proud* of having butchered the poor defenseless thing in cold blood.

"I was going to mount the head and hang it up," he muttered.

I felt like hanging *him* up.

"Bury it," I repeated.

"Where?" he asked sulkily.

"I don't care where, so it's away from here. Bury it in your own front garden, if you want to. And then come back here."

So he turned up again just as old AC—our sun—was setting, very sweaty and dirty and sullen. Digging a grave for a xenophere must be quite a chore.

"Now what?" he growled.

I'd been thinking while he was gone.

"Now," I said, "you turn some of that mighty prowess of yours into useful channels. I'm sending you to work in the library."

"The library!" He looked as if I'd condemned him to a dungeon.

"Sure. You don't have to read anything. There's plenty of heavy labor there, pushing trucks and scrubbing floors and things. But just to remind you that you're living in a civilized world, here's another requirement of your— shall we call it your probation? For the next eight weeks, the rest of the season, you're to attend the symphony concert every Sunday afternoon."

Then Johnny did look stricken, which was exactly how I wanted him to feel.

"But Sunday's my day for hiking!" he protested.

"Not for the next two months it isn't. You'll get plenty of exercise in the library. And maybe," I added meanly, "someday you'll stretch your brain enough to take a look at Dr. Mackinnon's book on the native fauna of Albia, and learn why we don't murder the animals that keep the prairies cropped against fire hazard and whose dung we collect for fertilizer on the organic farms."

It wasn't exactly making the punishment fit the crime, but at least it was making it fit the criminal.

"And the next time anything like this happens," I con- cluded, dismissing him, "I'll confiscate that bow and arrow of yours and destroy them—and heaven help you if you ever come up with another lethal weapon."

That did get him; he slunk out without another word. He was pretty good for a while after that—obeyed

orders, and the library and symphony hall both reported
he didn't miss a day. He knew he was being watched. I
began to think maybe we'd reformed our only case of
atavism.

Alas, you don't cure Johnny Newsons that easily.

He fell in love. Not the decent, mild way we fall in love
on Albia, leading to Permanent Partnership and, if both
desire it, sometimes a baby or two. Oh, no: Johnny Newson
in love was again a throwback, to the old bad days of
lust and jealousy and strutting *machismo*. And the object
of all this was of course no receptive young girl, but a
woman five years his senior and the wife of our venerated
Chief Medical Counselor.

Geraldine Trask was a small, fair-haired woman, slight
and graceful and looking younger than her years. But she
was no blonde nitwit; she was a senior accountant in the
Financial Administration Department. Unfortunately, computers meant more to her than suitors—besides, she was
quite contented with her gentle, dependable Malcolm.

So she made the bad mistake of treating Johnny Newson's advances as a joke.

She laughed about it everywhere—at home, in the office,
at every social gathering. It became the season's funniest
story. One of our popular singers made an amusing ballad
about it—"Oh, Johnny. Why?"—and we all bought the
record.

One might well ask how anybody so out of our style as
Newson should ever have found himself near enough to
the Chief Medical Counselor and his wife to bring such a
situation into being. The incident with the xenophere was
responsible for that. Naturally there was a scandal when
the dead beast was dragged through the public streets
of the settlement, and it was increased when as suddenly
the carcass disappeared. I made no secret of my ruling,
and Johnny became the day's whippingboy or laughing-
stock, according to the dispositions of the whippers or
laughers, in consequence. He took that well enough, having
been accustomed from infancy to both censure and ridicule,
but of course it all added to the store of angry rebellion
building up within him.

Several of our administrators and officials took the trouble to come to me and commend my handling of the case (much, I confess, to my gratification; I too, like all men and women, have my little vanities—moreover, I was running for reelection), but my old friend Dr. Trask went further. He proposed that he take Johnny Newson into his own household and undertake a course of psychological treatment aimed at transforming his erratic nature into one nearer the Albian norm.

Have I said that this young man had no one with natural ties or claims to agree or object? Indeed, though I am no expert in the sciences, my own field being sociology, I have often wondered if this were not the root cause of Johnny's strangeness. We are not much given to strict laws of matrimony, and there was no blame put on his mother or on him because his paternal ancestry was uncertain; but the mother herself, who died while he was still little more than a child, was an odd woman—not violent or obtuse like her son, but certainly not one of our scholars or intellectuals. She was an entertainer by profession, frequently on tour, and Johnny could be said to have been more dragged up than brought up. Not that a different childhood could have made him a different being, but even so . . .

But she did die early, and from that time on Johnny was a ward of the colony, which fed and clothed and housed and tried to school him, but could hardly take the place of even an unsatisfactory mother.

I still had custody of him, thanks to the xenophere affair, and I was only too glad to have him off my hands. So I accepted Dr. Trask's offer gratefully, and Johnny, with no choice, was handed over to him.

The rest, I presume, was to be expected—though never so dreadful an outcome.

How far the Chief Medical Counselor's treatment had progressed, or what effect, if any, it had so far had, I have no idea. To me, when I happened to run across him, Johnny Newson seemed still the same old Johnny—chipper and cocky and aggressive, but not such a fool that he carried defiance into obvious danger to his own well-being.

Everything changed for the worse after that cursed record came out. Johnny's infatuation with Geraldine Trask reversed itself instantly into outrage and hatred. He blamed her for the song—and of course she had inspired it by her ill-placed humor. There were angry scenes at the Trasks', which Geraldine countered with ridicule and Malcolm with cool logic—neither of which did anything to calm him. All this I learned too late; Dr. Trask's policy was one of personal responsibility and maintenance of privacy between doctor and patient, so Johnny's furious outbreaks remained unknown to the world outside.

You can imagine the public shock, therefore—and try to imagine my own—when one morning Geraldine Trask was waylaid between her home and her office and struck down by an assailant who attacked her from behind (the scene was a short cut across a secluded field high in weeds and bushes), then beat her savagely to death. It was the first murder in Albia's history since the chaotic early days. Only one human being among us could conceivably have been guilty. And Johnny had disappeared.

It is not easy to disappear on Albia, and least of all in the settlement. We are underpopulated still, so there is plenty of open country; but, on the other hand, there is no way out, and sooner or later hunger and thirst and the need for rest will have to bring a fugitive into the neighborhood of people all of whom are aware of his situation and prepared to cope with it. At least, this is theoretically the case; in actuality, since our earliest, wilder days I can think of no similar instance. In any event, though as Chief Guardian I sent deputies immediately to find out what they could, there was no trace of Johnny Newson. I spent more than one sleepless night wondering what we could do if or when we did find him; we have no such system of punishment for crime as tradition tells us once obtained on Earth, for, except for trifling peccadilloes, we have for many years had no real crime to punish.

Given so unaccountable a being as Newson, it was hard to speculate. If by some unthinkable chance I had committed a murder, I am certain that I could not have borne the guilt longer than it would have taken to expiate it by my own death. But no one could imagine Johnny Newson a suicide, or that guilt would bring him back to confess and submit to whatever we decided to do to him. He had gone entirely berserk, and we might as well be dealing with an animal with which we were unable to communicate. An animal, in addition, still evading capture, and probably armed.

I did what I could. Going through Johnny's few possessions in the Trask house, I found the bow and a stock of arrows, which I confiscated. There were other things there, the fruit of his leisure hours, which were incomprehensible to me but evidence of his tendency to fool about with wood and iron and try to conjure up weird appliances that nobody else could find a meaning or a use for—proof enough of his motor-mindedness. I suppose he never in his life had read a book voluntarily.

As you may imagine, poor Dr. Trask was desolate. Not that he displayed his grief, or paraded his feelings in the Newson style; as always, he was quiet, dignified, and in control of himself. But one could see how he had lost weight, and how pale he had become, with dark circles under his eyes from wakeful nights. I was seriously concerned lest somehow Newson might sneak back and avenge himself on Malcolm as he had done on Geraldine, but when I suggested placing a deputy in the house as a guard, Malcolm dismissed the idea with a wave of the hand. I felt that the failure of his psychological regimen was almost as painful a blow as the murder of his wife.

Or perhaps I am being unfair. As later events proved, Malcolm Trask was a husband before he was a physician. But of what he had in mind he gave no intimation to me or to anyone else. About a week after Geraldine's funeral he too disappeared—as suddenly and as impenetrably as had Johnny Newson.

The medical deputies, at my request, divided the Chief Medical Counselor's practice among them—temporarily, we all hoped. Luckily, it was not a time of much serious illness, and only the few patients undergoing psychological or hypnotic treatment really suffered, and they not ir-

remediably. Of course people gossiped—the theories ran
from Trask's own murder or suicide to a mere need to
go somewhere alone and recover from the shock and
strain—but I seemed to be the only one to suspect that
he had gone to find Johnny Newson—and I kept it to
myself. The idea of direct vengeance is simply alien to
our Albian way of thinking.

Nevertheless, I was right, though not altogether right.
Three weeks later Malcolm Trask drove into the settlement, and in the back seat of his chariot, bound up and
glowering, sat Johnny Newson like a bale of cotton ready
for pressing.

I was confused and confounded by this trussing up.
The Dr. Trask I knew would have persuaded Johnny to
come back with him, or come back without him. Yes,
even though he had killed Geraldine. Has this throwback, I wondered uneasily, started to infect the rest of
us—the best of us, like Malcolm Trask? I should have
known better.

Johnny sat mute and scowling. Trask's mouth was grim,
but the haunting pain had gone from his eyes. I looked
my questions.

"Call a deputy and take care of him," he said, with
a nod toward his captive. Johnny disposed of for the
moment—he refused to walk and it took two men to carry
him out—Trask and I adjourned to my office.

"Where did you find him? How?" We were hardly
seated before I had to ask, or burst.

"Where?" Trask said evenly. "In a cave up near the
top of the Malvern Hills, past the Epsom Forest. And
how? That's the advantage of psychological training." He
smiled tightly. "You people were all hunting for a human
criminal. I went after a wild animal."

He leaned forward earnestly.

"Don't you see? Johnny Newson isn't just an aberrant
member of our society here—he's a complete reversion
to the kind of savage who inhabited Earth in our bad
last days there—the kind our Founding Parents came
here to escape. Oh, he's human, all right—I'm not talk-

ing any romantic nonsense about werewolves or whatever
—but even without the conditioning that made Earthmen
what *they* became—without the crowding, the discrimina-
tion, the awful frustrations—by some quirk of the genes
(you remember his erratic mother, and who knows who
fathered him?) he is so constituted that actually he feels
at home with violence and war and hostility and self-
assertion. They are his natural element.

"All our reasonableness and placidity and intellectual
interests must have maddened him for years. I recognized
that, partially, when I took charge of him, but I was too
optimistic and too late. All I did"—he sighed deeply—
"was to implement the inevitable explosion. And the victim, first of his perverted 'love' and then of his rage, was
my poor Geraldine."

"You couldn't know that," I said hastily. A Chief
Medical Counselor blaming himself for failure was something I couldn't contemplate. "And now I need your
advice. What can we do with him?"

Malcolm Trask sat in silence, wrestling with his
thoughts. Then he said slowly, "You know what we
can't do. We have no courts, no prisons, certainly no
capital punishment. Yet we can't simply let him loose; he
is incurable.

"I could see your puzzlement when you found I'd tied
him up as I did. I had to: he'd come away without that
beastly weapon of his, but he was waiting for me with a
club he'd carved from a tree branch. Luckily, I'd expected
him to come out fighting, and I'd prepared myself. I
threw the water from my canteen in his face and while
he was momentarily blinded I tripped him and bound
him with the cord I'd brought along. It was a tussle—
he fought like a demon, but I finally got him into the
chariot."

"My men can handle him," I assured him. "So what
now? We can't keep him tied up forever."

"Exactly," he agreed. "So I have a suggestion."

"Let's have it.

"When is the next ship due here from Earth?"

"You know that as well as I do," I answered, be-wildered. "Once every three years, a supply and trading freighter carrying orders given to the previous one. Were you thinking of shipping him on?"

"Hardly," he said bitterly. "A Johnny Newson loose in the Air Fleets would attract his own kind and end up as an inter-galactic bandit. No: my idea was to deport him to our ancestral planet. That's where he belongs. He'll end up there in prison or killed, but that's the kind of life he was born to live."

"We can't," I objected. "We have no such treaty with Earth. No immigrants here, no returned Albians there—not that there's ever been a candidate for replanetation. That was the original treaty the Founding Parents put over, 253 of our years ago."

"I know that as well as you do," said Malcolm Trask testily. "So we use our brains. We know what Earth's like now—don't you ever vid your Intercommunication set? Overpopulation, pollution, endemic crime, eternal wars, political coups: what do you think they've done to the average level of Earth intelligence by now? Oh, they still have the technology—but mentally we're so far their superiors it's like psychologizing a baby.

"What is Johnny Newson's birth date?" he asked abruptly.

"How should I remember? I can find out."

"Do. And manipulate it so that nine months before that an Earth freighter was here."

"You mean—?"

"Leave it to me. When the next ship gets here, I'll see the captain. Before I'm through with him, he'll be absolutely convinced that Johnny is one of theirs—they still have the old patriarchal system.

"In other words, he never belonged here, and they can have him back."

"It might work. . . ."

"It will. And even Johnny will be delighted. He hates everything we stand for, and when I was working with him all he could talk about was how much better they do things in the Old Home."

"And what do we do with him meanwhile? It might be half a year yet."

Malcolm Trask stood up.

"Give him to me," he said. "I'll take him back in my household. A bit of sleep teaching, some ICSS. . . . Maybe I should have done that long ago, to quiet him down."

"ICSS?"

"Intercranial Self-Stimulation. Been going on for centuries—started on Earth long before we left. We introduce electrodes at the proper points in the brain, the subject pushes the button and lives in happy dreams. This isn't your field; you have no idea how many of our fellow citizens are walking around right now equipped with the means to live in Nirvana. How do you think we transformed ourselves so rapidly into the peaceful people we are? You've never needed it, so it's never come to your attention. No one likes to mention it about himself."

"But wait—if you can do that, why not cure Johnny Newson right here?"

"Why? Two reasons. One, we can make the melancholy happy, the timid self-confident, the narcoleptic wakeful, the reserved outgoing. But Newson's kind of aggressiveness has no cephalic point of origin; it's an inextricable part of his whole makeup. I can keep him quiet till we dump him, but I can't change him—I realize that now, too late —into a creature fit for our world here.

"And two—" his voice shook—"I don't want to live for the rest of my life face to face with the man who murdered my wife. You owe me that much."

"Yet you're willing to keep him with you until the ship comes," I marveled.

For the first time I saw Malcolm Trask weep, the tears welling in his eyes and spilling over.

"My Geraldine," he said, "was what they used to call a saint. Oh, yes, I know she made that one fatal error— she thought Johnny Newson's pursuit of her was funny, and said so, far and wide. But just before—just before she—"

He swallowed hard and went on.

"The very last night before she died, she said to me, 'Malcolm, I think I've done wrong to a poor unfortunate man. I'm sorry I made fun of Johnny; he can't help what he is. I want you to promise, whatever he does, that you'll keep on trying to help him.'

"So I'll help him still, the only way I can. We'll send him back to where he can function 'normally.' And I'll see to it that he'll be glad to go.

"Come with me now to wherever your deputies have him, and I'll give him a shot so we can unbind him safely. And while he's out, I'll introduce the first electrode. Till the ship arrives he can keep himself busy working on those contraptions of his."

As we left the office together, Dr. Malcolm Trask looked almost happy.

Johnny was true to himself to the end. When the next ship came after the one that had taken him away, I found it had the same captain. I had been reelected Chief Guardian, so I was still in a position of authority. I asked him how Newson was getting along on Earth.

He looked at me quizically.

"If our trade with you wasn't so profitable," he said curtly, "I'd tell you it was none of your business. No, I should never have let you put it over on me to allow that wild animal aboard my ship."

I ignored the offensive tone; I could see I had unwittingly touched a nerve.

"What do you mean?" I asked. "What happened?"

"Three days out, Newson pulled some crazy weapon he'd smuggled in with him, a sort of clumsy laser gun. I thought you people didn't go in for guns."

"We don't. He must have manufactured it himself." ("Working on his contraptions," indeed!)

"He tried to take over the ship. Open mutiny. *We* do go in for protecting ourselves. There was no choice: I had to shoot him down. We recycled the body as we do all waste.

"That's all of your Johnny Newson that ever got to Earth."

slide show

george r. r. martin

Becker was the second speaker on the program. So he waited patiently.

The man who preceded him was a doctor, the head of some sort of charity clinic in one of the undercities. Tall, gaunt, and elderly, he spoke in a droning monotone, and kept running his fingers nervously through his sparse gray hair. The audience, some thirty-odd plump upperlevel matrons, was trying hard to pay attention, but Becker could sense their restlessness.

He didn't blame them. The presentation wasn't very effective. The doctor was telling medical horror stories, of under-city kids too poor to get decent hospital care, of needless deaths, and of long-cured diseases that still flourished down below. But his voice and his manner drained the punch from his words. And his slides, as well as being of the old-fashioned flat kind, were woefully ill-chosen. Instead of moving photos of sick kids and undercity squalor, there were tedious pictures of the clinic and its staff, and then even blueprints of the proposed expansion.

Becker fought to stifle his own yawns. He felt a little

bit sorry for the doctor. But only a little bit. Mostly he was still feeling sorry for himself.

Finally the doctor concluded his presentation with a halting, self-conscious plea for funds. The ladies gave him a round of polite applause. Then the chairwoman turned to Becker. "Any time you're ready to begin, Commander," she said pleasantly.

Becker rose from his contour chair and flashed a plastic smile. "Thank you," he said, as he made his way to the front of the plushly furnished living room. He waited a moment while the doctor cleared the old slide projector from the speaker's table, then swung up his portable holocaster to take its place. "You can take down the screen, ladies," he said. "My machine doesn't need it. And clear a circle around—oh—there." He pointed.

The women hastened to comply. Becker watched them and smiled at them. But inside, as usual, he felt only a vague distaste for the whole thing.

Even in the darkened living room, he cut a much more imposing figure than the doctor, and he knew it. He was big and broad of shoulder, and the soft gray uniform he wore hinted at his athletic build. He had a classic profile, a decisive chin, and thick black hair with just a touch of gray at the temples. And his steel-blue eyes were perfectly matched by the leather of his boots and belt, and the scarf that was casually knotted about his neck, under the open collar.

He looked very much like a SPACE recruiting poster. Of late, he'd regretted that. There were times, in recent years, when he'd have given anything for a hook nose, or a weak chin, or a receding hairline.

The holocaster was set up and humming, and the audience was waiting. Becker pushed his thoughts aside and thumbed the first slide.

In the circle the women had cleared, a cube of deeper darkness appeared. Darkness touched by stars. In one corner of the cube, Earth floated in silent blue-green majesty. But the center of the holograph was occupied by the ship. A fat silver cigar with a pot belly. Or a pregnant torpedo. There were many ways to describe it, and most of them had been used at one time or other.

Appreciative murmurs sounded from the audience. The holoslide was very real, and very striking. Becker, smiling, began smoothly. "This is the *Starwind*, one of the four SPACE starcruisers. The cruisers are stellar exploration ships, each with a crew of more than a hundred. Antispacejump generators give them speeds many times that of light. These four frail ships, even as I speak, are carrying out the destiny of our race, and making man's age-old dream a reality. They are giving man the stars."

A practiced note of warm fondness crept into his voice, and he gestured at the silver shape afloat in the cube of black. "The *Starwind* was my ship," he said. "I was one small member of its crew during its last voyage. The slides you are about to see were taken during that voyage, a voyage that must rank among the most eventful in history. At least I'd say so." He smiled. "But then, I'm prejudiced."

His voice went on, detailing the size, design, and capabilities of the starcruiser and its crew. But he never got too technical, and there were always human touches and even hints of poetry to spice the presentation. Becker was too good at his job to bore *his* audience.

But even as his tongue went through its familiar paces, his mind was elsewhere. Out with the *Starwind*, in the sunless void of antispace. Out among the stars.

Where is she now? he thought. *It's been almost a year now since she left. On this new trip. Without me. God knows what new worlds they've found while I'm stuck back here, feeding slick crap to little old ladies.*

And there was an old bitterness to his thoughts, and an old longing in his stomach. And he grew aware, for the millionth time, of how much he hated what his life had become. But no hint of that crept into his smooth and warm and very professional speech.

He thumbed the holocaster, and the slide changed. Now the cube was blinding white, flecked with pits of pulsing black. And in the center of the projection was a thing that looked like a floating black octopus with glowing crimson veins.

"This is antispace," Becker said simply. "Or at least, this is how human eyes perceive antispace. The mathematicians are still trying to figure out its true nature. But when our jump-generators are on, this is how we see it. Almost like a photographic negative: white darkness, and sparkling black stars."

He paused, waiting for the inevitable question. And, as always, it came. "Commander," one of the women said, "what's that—that *thing* in the middle?"

He smiled. "You're not the only one who'd like to know," he said. "Whatever it is, it has no counterpart in normal space. Or at least, none that we can see. But it and things like it have been sighted several times by starcruisers in antispace. This slide, taken by the *Starwind* on its last voyage, is the best picture we've ever gotten of one. The creature—if it is a creature, which is still only a guess—is larger than a ship. By a good deal. But it seems to be harmless."

His voice was reassuring. His mind wondered. *Seems to be harmless,* he thought. *Yeah. But this one seemed to be after the ship. There are still arguments about whether it could have done anything if it caught us. Maybe this time it did. Maybe it got them this trip. I always said it was possible. Although the brass doesn't like to admit it. They're afraid that there'll be more budget cuts if they admit the program is dangerous. So they pretend that everything is safe and sane and bland out there, just like Earth. But it isn't. It isn't. Earth died of dullness years ago. Out there a man can still live, and feel, and dream.*

He finished his spiel on antispace. His thumb moved. The cube of white vanished. Instead, a huge red globe burned in the center of the room.

"The *Starwind's* first stop was this red giant, still unnamed," Becker told the women. "The crew nicknamed it Red Light. Because it stopped us. And because it *is* a red light, rather obviously. There were no planets, but we circled this star for a month, taking readings and sending in probes. The information we gathered should tell us a lot about stellar evolution."

I remember the first time I saw it, he was thinking as

he spoke. *God! What a sight! My first star—Sol doesn't count. Wilson was on watch with me, but he was so damned busy taking readings he hardly bothered to look. Yet now he's out there again. And I'm here. There's no justice. . . .*

A new slide. This time a mottled globe of orange and blue floated in the cube. Behind it, a bright yellow sun only slightly smaller than Sol.

Becker's voice became solemn. "Our first planetfall," he said. "And one of the greatest moments in human history. That is the planet we named Anthill. I'm sure you've read all about it by now, and seen the holoshows. But remember, for us it was new and strange and unexpected. This was humanity's first contact with another sentient race."

He thumbed for the next slide, one of the big ones. And when it flashed into view, there were the expected gasps of awe and admiration. The audience held its collective breath.

There was a vast, dark plain in the center of the cube, under a blood-red sky where scuttling black clouds obscured the alien sun. And rising from the plain, the towers. Thin and black and twining, twisting around each other, branching together and splitting again as they rose. They rose for nearly a mile, and all around them were the fragile weblike bridges that linked each to its brothers to make an intricate whole. A river ran through the middle of the city, and gave a clue to the vast size of the structure.

"One of their cities," Becker said. And the slight note of awe in his voice was real. "The home of more than a million of them, by our estimate. We called the builders Spiderants. Because there was something of the spider web in the cities that they built. And because—well, look."

The city vanished. The new slide was a closeup. A thick black strand looping through the cube. From it hung what looked like a four-foot-long ant. But appearances were deceiving.

There were a few murmurs of revulsion, even though most of the audience had probably seen photos before. Becker quelled them quickly. "Don't be fooled," he cautioned. "Despite what your eyes tell you, that's not a big ant. It's not even an insect. No exoskeleton, for example, although it looks like one at first glance. And that bug, we think, is quite intelligent. Their culture is very different from ours. But they have their own sense of beauty. Look at their city again."

He touched his holocaster. The hanging Spiderant vanished, and again the towers rose amid the carpet. The same angle. But this time, night. And it made a difference.

For the towers glowed.

Black in the reddish daylight, now they shone with a soft green light. A gorgeous glowing tracery against the darkness, they rose and rose and twisted, and every loop and web had a soft radiance all its own. Unbelievably intricate.

Becker, despite himself, still shivered at the slide. As he had shivered the first time he had seen it. In person. The holo woke dreams and memories, and made him hate his reality all the more.

They've taken this away from me, he thought. *Forever. And given me—what? Nothing. Nothing I want, anyway.*

But he said only, "And when the dawn comes . . ." And the slide changed.

Now a reddish-yellow glow suffused the horizon behind the city, and the radiance of the towers was paler and dying. But something new, and just as awesome, had been added. For now the web of the city was aswarm with life. From each branch and strand and loop, Spiderants hung. Dangling even from the highest towers, nearly a mile above the ground. Clustered together, crawling over each other, yet somehow orderly. The whole city.

"They do this every dawn," Becker said. "And as their sun rises, they sing to it."

If you can call it song, he thought. *To my ears, that first night outside the landing craft, it was moaning. But weird. Rising and falling, up and down, for hours and hours. Even Wilson was awestruck. A million beings moaning together, moaning a hymn to their sun.*

His thumb flicked down and up, and suddenly they were looking at a closeup of a web strand, laden heavy with Spiderants. Then it moved once more, and there was another view of the city. And after a while still another, and another. And all the time his voice went on, telling of this curious race and the little they had learned about it.

"The *Starwind* lay off Anthill for more than six months, sending down landing craft regularly," he said. "But the Spiderants are yet a race of unanswered questions. We still have not cracked their language, or determined how intelligent they really are. They seem to have no technology, as we know it. But they have—well—something else."

More views of the city came and went. And then of other, like cities. And some not so like—one that rose from the planet's brackish sea, and another where the towers jutted sideways to join two mountains in a twisted embrace.

"We had been there nearly a month before we were allowed up in the towers," Becker continued. "And even then it took us a while before we realized that the cities of the Spiderants were not built, but grown. Those towers are not buildings at all. They are plants: huge, incredibly hardy, incredibly complex. But, for all that, plants."

Lawrence was the first one to find that out, he remembered. *He was so damned excited when he got back that he was incoherent. But he had a right to be. It was our first clue. Before that, nothing made sense. Mile-high towers without machines were especially nonsensical. At least I thought so. Hell. I wonder where Lawrence is now.*

"When we discovered that, we began to wonder whether the Spiderants were intelligent after all. We got our answer when we branched out from the original landing site. This was one of the things we saw."

Red-black gloom suddenly filled the cube. Through it flapped something huge and green and triangular. Airborne and manta-like, with a long tail that split in half over and over again until it was a trail of thin, whiplike tendrils.

Far below it, a city. On top, Spiderants.

"This is a domesticated flying creature, almost as big as a jet. It has to stay low, of course, And it doesn't have anything like an airplane's speed. But then, it doesn't pollute, either. And it gets around."

We got around faster, though, he thought. *I remember that afternoon I trailed one with a flyer. God, but those things are slow. Still, sort of majestic. And when those incredible wings flap with that funny rippling motion, it's something to see. Of course, that ass Donway had to try buzzing it. At least he's down, too. I couldn't stand it if he had gone out again.*

"What it is, of course," he was saying, "is another plant. A mobile, flying plant. When it's not transporting Spiderants, it flies up high to catch the sun. And it takes in nourishment through that tail structure, which is actually a root of sorts. A lot more complicated than anything any Earth plant has, of course."

He went through several more slides, showing other mantas, and then several of them in formation. "We think that these things were bred deliberately by the Spiderants. As were the towers. If the theory is right, then we've stumbled across the greatest biological engineers you could ever want. There's a lot to be learned from them, if we can crack the communications barrier. Anthill will be a regular stop for our starcruisers from now on."

Including the Starwind, *of course. She was scheduled to visit there again this mission. Maybe she's there now. Maybe Lawrence and Wilson and the rest are listening to the Spiderants right this moment. While I talk. Or sing. My performance doesn't much compare to theirs.*

He paused. "We spent more than six months on Anthill, and had to cut out much of our scheduled mission because of the overstay. But I think you'll agree that it was worth it"—with a smile, and the ladies in the audience mumbled agreement. "Finally, however, we had to move on. There was still time for one more stop before we turned around and began to jump for home."

He hit the button, and the last view of Anthill died. The holo that was born in its stead was spectacular. The matrons greeted it with gasps. They'd seen it before, on magazine covers and news broadcasts. But the holoslide captured more, much more.

"The world we called Storm," Becker said. Very softly. And then fell silent while they looked.

A surly green sea was wrestling the wind. From it rose the volcano: a trident in bluish-black stone whose triple peaks dripped fire. Smoke whipped up to mix with the glowering sky, lava coiled down to stream hissing into the ocean.

And *above* the volcano, literally leaning over it, a foam-flecked wall of green. Tidal wave? No. The Earth term didn't apply. This was bigger. More spectacular. Looming larger than the mountain itself, caught just seconds before impact.

"We couldn't land on Storm," Becker said. "There was no safe place to put down. But we sent manned probes into the atmosphere. This slide was taken by one of those probes." He smiled again and put a note of pride into his voice. But in with the pride, just barely, was a taste of anger. "I'm happy to tell you that it was my probe."

At least they can't take that away from me, he thought. *They took away my stars, but they can't take Storm. I captured it with this picture. The essence of a planet. The soul. There, in a holocube. And it's mine.*

And I was the only one to see the rest. Seconds after. When the wildwave hit, and the volcano broke and shattered under the blow, and the world was full of storm and steam and fire. And I was the only one to watch. . . .

His voice was going on smoothly without him. "Storm is a young world," it was saying. "Still very much a toddler on the celestial scale. But it's a lusty kid. It's mostly water, and what land there is is still volcanic. Earthquakes and eruptions are daily events—and they give birth to things like the wildwave you see in the cube. Winds average hundreds of miles an hour, and the electrical displays make common Earth lightning look pale and weak. Look."

The trident and the wildwave vanished, and a skyscape took their place. There was ball lightning everywhere, and massive bolts that crackled and joined in a blinding net.

You can almost hear the thunder just looking at it. But on Storm, I didn't just hear. I felt it. It was all around

*me, and the ship shook to it, and I was scared shitless.
But at least I was alive. What am I now?*

His thumb moved of its own volition, and a new view
of Storm came oncube. And his voice continued its glib
narration. But the rest of him was millions of miles away,
lost in a land of lightning and wildwaves.

Storm was my favorite, his thoughts ran. *Red Light was
a heart-stopping first, and Anthill was haunting and
puzzling and magical. But them I shared. Storm was
almost my own. Only a handful of us got to swoop down,
after Ainslie got careless and let his probe get blown
against a mountain. But I was one of the handful. They
can't take that away, either.*

His mind wandered. But all the while new vistas came
and went in the cube, and his voice went on, and the
ladies ooohed and aahed on schedule. And, finally, the
end approached. And jerked him back to reality.

The next-to-last slide was the same as the first; the
Starwind, in orbit around Earth. Waiting for new supplies,
and new funding, and a new mission. And a few new men.

The last slide was an address. Glowing red letters
floated in the white cube. And Becker, hating it, provided
the narration.

"Space exploration is the greatest adventure in man's
history," he said, smiling his plastic smile and talking with
a plastic-pleasant tongue. "And the stars are our joy and
our destiny. Not everyone can go to the stars, of course.
But all those who want to can share in the adventure, and
help to build the destiny. Worldgov has many expenses,
and many causes crying for priority. It can only fund a
small part of the budget needed to operate the starcruisers.
The rest, as you know, is provided by interested citizens.

"If you share our dreams, we ask you to join the fight.
For only a hundred credits a year, you can become members of the Friends of SPACE. You'll receive membership
credentials, of course. And a complimentary subscription
to *Starflight,* the official SPACE magazine. And you'll be
giving a gift to your children. *All* your children, and all
the children of man. You'll be giving them the stars.

"For a gift like that, the price tag is pretty low." He

pointed at the address floating in the holocube. "If you'd like to help, send your contributions there—to SPACE, Box 27, Worldgov Center, Geneva."

His smile broadened. "And, of course, all contributions are tax deductible." He bowed silently, and flicked off the holocaster. "Whether you care to contribute or not, I hope you enjoyed the show."

Then the audience started applauding, and the lights came on, and the chairwoman rose to announce that refreshments would be served. While they were getting the food, a steady stream of women flowed up to Becker and thanked him effusively for his presentation and promised him support. He acknowledged their praise with nods and laughter and pleasant smiles.

And despised them, all the while. *God,* he thought, *I hate this. They've taken away my stars and given me chattering fat ladies and phony upperlevel parlors. And I hate it. And it isn't fair. Hell, it isn't even life.*

They gave him synthetic coffee and protein cookies. And he took them with a smile. And hated them. But he ate them, and stayed, and made small talk. That was SPACE policy. Finally, the audience began to break up and leave, one by one.

Just as Becker was beginning to think of leaving, the doctor drifted up, holding his coffee limply. He didn't seem quite as old with the lights on. But he looked very tired.

"That was quite a show, Commander," he said with a wan smile. "I'm afraid you blitzed me. I have a hunch you'll be getting all the contributions."

Becker returned a professional smile. "Well, your own presentation was very interesting, Doctor. And there's certainly a need for your kind of work down in the undercities. I wouldn't be so pessimistic."

The doctor frowned slightly, sipped his coffee, and shook his head. "Come, Commander. Don't humor me. I'm new at this game and I did very badly. And you're good enough to know that."

Becker, who was busy packing up his holocaster, gave the doctor a sharp glance and a genuine grin. He looked around to make sure none of the women were in range of the conversation, then nodded quickly. "You're sharp. And right—your show was third-rate. But you'll get better with time. And then the contributions will start to come in."

"Hmmmm. Yes." The doctor looked at him hard, paused. Then he seemed to make up his mind about something. And he continued. "Meanwhile, of course, thousands of kids down in the undercities are hungry and sick. And they stay that way. And maybe die. Why? Because I'm not as slick as you." His mouth set in a hard line. "Tell me honestly, Commander—don't you ever feel guilty?"

The case on the holocaster snapped up with a sharp click, and Becker's grin died. "No," he said. There was a bite in his tone suddenly. "Doctor, you know that there are four starcruisers. There could be forty. Or four hundred. There should be. But Worldgov won't give us the money. Comments like you just made are costing us the stars."

Are costing me the stars, he was saying to himself, his mind seething. *So few ships, so many volunteers. And that damned waiting list . . .*

What was it that General Henderson had said? Thousands, wasn't it? Yes. "Commander, there are thousands of applicants for every starcruiser berth. And your performance on your first voyage was . . . well, adequate. But not outstanding. I'm afraid I'm going to have to turn down your application for permanent crew status. I'm sorry."

And I said . . . what? I said, "You're taking away my stars." For the first time, if not the last.

"I'm sorry," he said. That bastard. He never flew on a starcruiser in his life. That fatass would never leave Earth. "There's nothing I can do. However, Commander, there's still a place for you. You're good-looking and articulate, and you believe in what we're doing. SPACE needs men like you. We're moving you to public relations. Without which, I might add, the starcruisers would be impossible."

"I'm as compassionate as anyone," Becker said, slinging the holocaster under an arm. "I think your work is vital. I feel for those kids. But you should try some empathy too.

And try to understand what we're doing."

"What you're doing is a luxury when kids are hungry on Earth," the doctor said.

Becker shook his head. "No. There has to be room for both. Say you save a kid from death, Doctor. Fine. But what kind of life are you giving him? A pretty drab one, without the stars. And a hopeless one, in the long run. Maybe man can survive on Earth, alone. I think he could. But his dreams can't, and his myths can't. There are too many people, and they've crowded out all the dreams. And there's no life left for anyone. Just day-to-day survival."

He paused there. It was good speech, his own restatement of arguments he had heard hundreds of times in SPACE headquarters. It was enough. But he wanted to add more. He was angry and resentful, and he went on.

"I'll tell you something else, Doctor. I think we need both your work and mine, both Earth and the stars. But I think the balance is wrong. I think we need more stars."

He slapped the holocaster with his free hand. "You think I *like* this sort of shit? I hate it, Doctor. Just like you'd hate it if you did it all the time. I've dreamed of the stars all my life, and now they tell me I'm not good enough to get a permanent berth on a starcruiser. Not that I'm bad, mind you. I'm just not outstanding enough. And there's so little room.

"Tell me, Doctor, how would you feel if Worldgov suddenly announced that only the *best* four hundred doctors in the world would be allowed to practice medicine? Would you make the grade? What would you do? Can you imagine what it'd be like? Going through life, day to day, knowing what you wanted to do—and knowing that it was denied to you, maybe forever. Try to imagine that, if you can. Try to taste it. That's what it's like for me, you see.

"You can't *live* on Earth, Doctor. *I* can't, anyway. I can exist, but I don't call it living. I've seen the wild-waves of Storm and listened to the Spiderants sing their dawn. Am I supposed to content myself with mindspin trips and football games?" He snorted.

The doctor had calmly continued to sip his coffee during Becker's outburst. Now he lowered his cup, sighed, and gave another tired shake of his head.

"Commander, I feel sorry for you," he said. "You sound very bitter. Like you've been cheated. But you've been so incredibly lucky. And you don't realize it. You've done things most people only dream of, yet you complain of an empty life. I don't buy that. You've flown on a star-cruiser, even if it was only once. Commander, let me tell you something. Down in the undercity I've got patients who've never even *seen* the stars. And you've been there."

Becker, his anger subsided, gave a wistful smile that seemed somehow out of character. But very genuine.

"I've thought of that," he said sadly. "Sometimes. Maybe you're right. But it doesn't help, Doctor. I wish it did. But it doesn't." He thought a minute. "I'm sorry for your patients who've never seen the stars," he said when he resumed. "You know, I think that's almost worse than hunger. Although that's not fair for me to say, since I've never really been hungry. I hope someday you take your kids to the upperlevels, so they get a glimpse through the smog."

Becker shrugged then. "They're not the only ones I'm sorry for, though. I'm sorry for everyone who has seen the stars and can't go there. And most of all I'm sorry for me, who's been there. And can't go back. I guess that makes me selfish. But that's the way it is, I'm afraid. And I try to live with it.

"And I do sort of believe in what I do. Maybe someday Worldgov will change its mind and we'll get more starcruisers. And I can go out again. And take some of your kids with me, who knows? It's for them too, you know."

Becker wanted to end it there. But the doctor, still un-convinced, came back again. "That's big of you," he said. "But before you give them the stars, try giving them some food, or a healthy environment."

Becker glanced around the room. It was very late, and most of the audience had gone home. *Time to break it off*, he thought. *Another damned show tomorrow.*

"I could answer that," he said. "But I won't. I'm not going to convince you, Doctor. And you're not going to convince me, either, I'm afraid. So let's call it a night. Peace?"

He smiled and offered his hand. The doctor shook it. Then Becker turned to the chairwoman and the few matrons who remained, and bade them good night. And left.

It was cold outside on the upperlevels, and there was a brisk night wind whistling down the street between the towertops. Becker stopped briefly on his way to the inter-level tubes and looked up. But the smog was heavy, and he could not see the stars.

And maybe that was just as well.

rabble-dowser

anne mc caffrey

"And all indications point to this campus next."

Berstock's outrageous statement was so at variance with his meek appearance and credentials that William Barry Rentnor, president of Cavaye College, was tempted to laugh in the man's face. And throw him and his moronic companion out of the office. These were critical days for Cavaye and even the mere thought of a riot . . .

"Really, Dr. Berstock, how could Cavaye be next on this so-called riot list of yours? We're a growing institution, yes, but—"

"And you also anticipate awards from ISACA and the Vibeke Pharmaceutical Corporation?"

Rentnor stared at the man in astonishment, for the very whisper of those coveted grants was a secret confined to Rentnor and the Board of Directors of Cavaye College.

"Time and again, Dr. Rentnor," Berstock continued inexorably, "riots have occurred prior to such grants and awards, almost as if some agency—other than the students themselves—was trying to prejudice the committees against those particular institutions."

98

Rentnor allowed his disbelief to show in his face. "Really, Dr. Berstock, not the Commies again. And if it were not for funds from industrial and government sources, colleges like Cavaye would quickly go bankrupt."

"Understood, Dr. Rentnor, understood." Berstock raised a placating hand.

"To be sure, Cavaye has its dissident minority," Rentnor said, determined to wind up this unproductive interview. Berstock was quite presumptuous and yet . . . "Cavaye has its dissident minority, but basically they're a law-abiding group and—"

"No one knows *what* triggers a law-abiding group—" and Berstock smiled with gentle emphasis—"into a raving destructive mob. Nor why grown men would fire live bullets at a group of students."

"Cavaye is not Kent State."

"Agreed. We are just beginning to appreciate the mechanics of mob psychology—what pressures, stimuli, what—"

"And you are trying to convince me that . . . that . . ." Rentnor's irritation abruptly doubled as he glanced toward the moron.

"His name is Jeremy Goslin," Berstock said with firm courtesy.

"This . . . this Mr. Goslin . . ." Rentnor broke off because the moron's previously stupid, passive features were the classic picture of irritability, from deep scowl to thin lips.

"I can see that my announcement and the rationale behind my theory perturbs you, Dr. Rentnor."

"Perturb me? My dear Berstock, I am not perturbed by whimsical fancies and . . ." Rentnor's voice trailed off because he could not continue in the presence of Goslin's reaction. That was exactly the way he felt.

"My dear Dr. Rentnor, I'd believe you if Jeremy were not here, broadcasting your real emotions."

Rentnor was on his feet, smiling pleasantly but with firm dismissal in his manner. "Dr. Berstock, you presume on my time, intelligence, and patience."

Goslin began to breathe so stertorously that Rentnor's

attention was again diverted to him.

"I'd better have Jeremy wait outside while we talk," Berstock said, and before Rentnor could muster a protest, the other man had coaxed the panting, distressed Goslin out of the office. "Jeremy's a bit upset, miss," he said to Rentnor's surprised secretary. "Would you smile at him as if you were very glad to see him and very fond of him? As soon as he smiles back, you can forget about him and resume your filing. Sit down here, Jeremy."

Dumfounded by Berstock's tactic, Rentnor had a brief glimpse of his secretary's startled but obediently smiling face as Berstock closed the door firmly behind him.

"If my presentation dispenses with certain courtesies, Dr. Rentnor, I apologize. Jeremy's reflection of your aggravation and annoyance validates my contention that he is an emotional barometer. You can surely recognize the true moron when you see one. You certainly know that such a mentality . . . rather the lack of it . . . in general cannot respond with such immediacy to ordinary stimuli. We've been in your office a bare five minutes, and in my brief summation of purpose and aim I paid no attention to Jeremy at all, gave him no signals which could have resulted in his display of emotion. And if I should open the door right now, you would see Jeremy smiling happily at your secretary. Or possibly frowning if she can't find the right file."

The quiet voice, the confident words, the utter conviction of Berstock forced Rentnor to master his temper.

"If you wish to verify my credentials, you are at liberty to do so, but please do it immediately. We don't have much time. Less than I thought we had, to judge by Jeremy's reactions to the various groups we passed on our way to this building."

Rentnor glanced apprehensively out the wide bay window that looked down the tree-shaded quadrangle. It was close to noontime and therefore large groups of students on the paths or lounging on the grass were by no means abnormal.

"We have styled Jeremy a telempath," said Berstock, "although a student wit named him a 'rabble-dowser.'"

Berstock gave a tight smile. "He's been with us since his early teens, when the damage to the frontal lobes of his brain was first discovered. Each day, each hour is a brand-new experience for Jeremy. His only consistent response is to the various emotions which he encounters. Encounters, measures, and reacts to. He is really a human barometer. Put him in the room with someone violently depressed, very happy, euphoric on drugs, irritated, angry—as you were—wildly in love, paranoidal, anxious, tearful, and Jeremy will reflect that emotion instantly."

Rentnor could not help but speculate. The two committees, ISACA and the Vibeke governors, were even now deciding which of the several colleges and universities would be awarded grants. He'd confidently told his own Board of Directors that at least Cavaye had a law-abiding student body and this would weigh heavily for—or disastrously against—Cavaye in the final analysis. If he could just keep Cavaye trouble-free . . .

"All you've told me may be perfectly true, Dr. Berstock, but tell me, if Jeremy Goslin is such a trustworthy gauge, why did City College—"

"Come off it, Dr. Rentnor," Berstock replied with startling colloquial directness. "The larger the university, the harder it is to get them to move quickly. Unfortunately, by the time we realized Jeremy's potential, the situation had exploded. We did rout out the leaders and scare them off."

"With Jeremy?" Rentnor was taken aback. The moron was physically big, but to loose on any unsuspecting victims such a mindless juggernaut, primed with riotous emotions . . . Rentnor stopped. The notion of Jeremy loose among the sour anarchists had a certain appeal. Those dissidents made corrosive weapons of logic and debate, made a shambles of candor, and vandalized conservatism. If only the holes they made in the fabric of the status quo looked out on greener pastures or happier prospects . . .

"We used Jeremy as a rabble-dowser," Berstock continued, "and it was not hard for us to find the point from which the riot had generated. We took the appropriate steps."

Rentnor looked at Berstock's calm face, scarcely crediting his ears. Such a man, with academic degrees from top universities, with professional honors, exploiting a moron in such a bizarre pursuit!

"Come, Rentnor. You're calmer now. Grant me—at least on the basis of my credentials, on Goslin's reaction to your suppressed irritation, his foolish smile for your secretary—that he does respond to emotion as I have said. Then take a walk with me, Jeremy between us, through that quadrangle and observe. Believe me," and Rentnor caught a glimpse of anxiety hidden behind Berstock's quiet mien, "no one will be more relieved than I if my riot-dowser evinces no reaction at all. I can be on my way to see if I can help another university that seems in great danger too."

Rentnor masked a wince at the "too." The man was patently sincere. If he were also accurate in his assessment of the situation at Cavaye . . . and could thwart a budding demonstration . . .

"Answer me one question, Berstock. Why Cavaye? Why not State College with its larger minority groups and a history of student dissensions? Why not the big men's college at South—"

"Because the disease is just starting here. It's already too late for what Jeremy can do at State College and the other one. But it's just started here."

Fleetingly Rentnor wondered if Berstock was slightly paranoid. Those riots at his university had been viciously prolonged: students had been hospitalized, and hadn't one been trampled to death? Hadn't the Psych Building been isolated and in a state of siege for several days?

"I've had the student papers from every college and university airmailed to me," Berstock said, "once we realized what we had in Jeremy. We've analyzed the tactics of the dissenters. They follow a pattern. The exact chronology is unpredictable because each institution is at a different level of 'boil' since the Columbia riots. But the tactics are basically the same. The start is innocent. The deans don't realize that their tolerance and permissiveness only fertilize the soil in which riots grow. . . . But I'm wasting time."

Jeremy was sitting, smiling inanely at nothing, because the secretary had left the office.

"Come, Jeremy, we're taking a walk," Berstock said in the patient tone in which he invariably addressed his ward.

The hulk that was Jeremy Goslin rose obediently and let itself be guided to the door. The portraits of distinguished past presidents in gilt frames smiled benignly at their progress down the wide parquet corridor to the double-doored entrance. The brilliant spring sunlight poured through the unusual Georgian fanlight, glancing off the recently painted walls. Which reminded Rentnor that the Student Council had petitioned to have their traditional assembly hall repainted this year. It needed it, Rentnor had admitted candidly, but he felt that the funds would be better spent in maintaining the Administration Building's image. The students had responded with a paint-in and Rentnor wondered if the resultant grievance contributed to the heated irrationalities reportedly bouncing off those lurid walls. He wished now that he'd approved the original request.

The three men were all in step down the worn granite stairs, three well-pressed left knees raised, extended, three shining shoe toes visible on the step below, three right knees bending back, lifting forward. They passed the row of cherry trees, which were at their best. Tomorrow, however, if this heat continued, the blossoms would be dropping off. Still, for their brief days of full costume, the trees were treasured by the maintenance men and the publicity office. Invariably the catalogue showed some view of the trees in full bloom.

Reluctantly Rentnor's eyes left the trees and went from the groups of students to fasten on Jeremy Goslin's loutish face. Rentnor wondered if one of the campus wits might intimate that Cavaye was scraping the bottom of the barrel to meet its promised quota.

"Could we go past the Mathematics Building, Dr.

Rentnor?" asked Berstock as they came to the triangle of paths at the concrete apron before the Administration Building. "I believe that your Math Department head has come in for some student criticism lately for his remarks about black mathematicians."

Rentnor suppressed his groan. Berstock knew entirely too much about what Rentnor had hoped had been *contained* on campus. Stefan Lenczi was a brilliant Hungarian, a mathematician's mathematician, and a feather in Cavaye's faculty cap. He was also a stubborn-minded man. He'd been flayed by the campus newspapers for a statement about the mathematical abilities/aptitudes of various ethnic groups. He had given a definitive opinion, with statistical proof, that there were no pure Negro mathematicians. He had stated that it was a problem of background, as it would be for anyone in the same position as the ethnically pure black, who had had no culture (by Western standards) or written language until 1850. Consequently Lenczi had been attacked as a racist. This he denied with equal vehemence.

"And you think we'll have a problem there?" Rentnor asked Berstock. Somehow that seemed the least likely possibility.

"I sincerely hope not," Berstock replied.

Unfortunately, one had to pass between Harley Hall and Breslaw to get to the Math quadrangle. Breslaw was the headquarters for the student-directed activities.

And yet . . . the first students they passed on their way were obviously not of the radical element: clean-clothed, the boys' hair no longer than their collars, the girls' faces shiny without makeup. All seemed to be listening to a funny story, for there were half-smiles on most of the faces. The narrator glanced up as the trio passed, nodding a polite acknowledgment of the president before his eyes slid to Rentnor's companions, without visible interest.

Rentnor glanced at Jeremy Goslin. The stolid face was expressionless, though Berstock unobtrusively slowed his pace as they passed the group.

Rentnor began to feel more confident. If Berstock's

rabble-dowser could give Cavaye a clean bill of health . . .

Loud noise preceded a quintet which swarmed out of Breslaw's Gothic-arched main door. Rentnor recognized several of the more aggressive student leaders: Colvano, Hedwar and his wild-haired leman (Rentnor had started academic life as a Chaucerian scholar) Johnson, and Medwick. His apprehension was immediately telegraphed to Goslin, and Berstock gave Rentnor a quizzing look.

"Yes, they're some of the more vocal students."

Colvano and Medwick saw Rentnor, but gave no sign of acknowledgment. Rather their arguments, conducted chorally, rose in volume and intensity. Fortunately, for the quintet seemed headed in the same general direction, they paused to concentrate on argument rather than locomotion.

"That's the student activity hall?" Berstock asked. "Which wasn't painted this year?"

"Do you know everything?"

"I try to research properly. And the matter was touched on in the student newspaper, the *Cavayan*. I might add that the comment was that the administration saw fit to renovate only those areas which would look well to occasional power-bloc and industrial visitors. The implication being that Cavaye plays too much politics."

Rentnor remembered the article all too vividly now. The reference to the painting had been insignificant compared to other accusations which still rankled deeply. If the college were to get the grants, it would have to expand its facilities and its campus. The only college properties suited to the proposed expansion happened to be low-income housing units on the south side.

" 'Down, not out' " had been the students' solution. And had cited the logic of subterranean expansion housing computer units, laboratories, and storage space, which were part of the college's crushing expansion needs.

"Surely," Rentnor said with, he felt, unforced geniality, "you can't mean to suggest that Cavaye is in imminent danger of riot and rebellion for the lack of a coat of paint?"

"I'll spare you the old cliché about the infamous nail, Dr. Rentnor, but you fail to realize that these demonstrations are just as effectively primed by a relatively insignificant issue as by an honest grievance. I have studied the pre-explosion atmosphere of many colleges and a pattern has emerged. Cavaye is at the threshold of that very predictable and unfortunate sequence of events."

Rentnor stopped. "Are you unalterably convinced that these riots are not spontaneous? That they are planned? Geared? Part of a massive conspiracy?"

Berstock waited until a group of students had passed them, for they were suddenly a stationary island in a general flow across the larger quadrangle.

"If you wish to undermine a society, you attack its safeguards: the police force and the places of learning. I need hardly cite the problems which beset the law-enforcement agencies or the institutions which are supposed to train up the responsible citizenry that will one day inherit the reins of government."

"Communists? Fascists?" Rentnor was both skeptical and contemptuous of such sources.

"You can scarcely deny that left-wing groups with elitist tendencies are active on campuses today."

Jeremy began to shuffle his feet nervously on the asphalt path, his eyes wide and white.

Rentnor took a deep breath, trying to suppress the rising agitation, but Berstock held up a warning hand.

"He's not reacting to you, Dr. Rentnor."

The soft words were ominous, and at Berstock's gesture Rentnor looked around at the tree-shaded quadrangle with its ivy-hung buildings and crisscrossing paths, paths too heavily populated right now.

"The Mathematics Building is in that direction?" asked Berstock.

"Yes." Apprehension lent a snap to Rentnor's pace. Then he saw MacCrate, one of the campus cops, coming from behind the Library on an interception course.

"Dr. Lenczi phoned me, sir. He tried to reach you."

"He did?" Rentnor's hand went to his breast pocket, where he kept his bleeper, an item which an electronic student had constructed for him to be in touch with his office and the campus police at all times. Rentnor felt it helped him also recall that the dissidents were the minority, and that many students were irritated by the protests, rallies, and sporadic interruptions of their study programs.

"He didn't tell your secretary it was urgent. But it is now. There's a large congregation outside his office. Shall I call—"

"It is vitally important not to precipitate a clash between students and authority," Berstock said quickly. "This may be a peaceful congregation which can lead to a calm, rational discussion of the issues." His eyes entreated Rentnor. "If you'd lead the way, perhaps we are in time to stop trouble at Cavaye."

"Trouble?" asked MacCrate, his glance shifting from Jeremy Goslin's blinking eyes and troubled face to his employer's. "Shall I . . ." and he reached for his own communications unit.

"No, no!" Berstock was insistent. "The presence of uniformed authority is often the final gust of wind that sets the kindling ablaze."

MacCrate looked in bewilderment from the college president to his companion.

"Alert the campus force, MacCrate, and stay within call of the Math Building."

"Now, it may be completely innocuous," Berstock told Rentnor as they strode quickly down the last few hundred yards that separated the quadrangles.

Lenczi was visible the moment they turned the corner by the Library. The Math Building was American Colonial, with wide windows across the front. The center one on the left-hand side was thrown wide open. Lenczi stood there, in his customary shirt sleeves, green plastic visor askew on his forehead, fists on his hips, listening.

Rentnor glanced apprehensively at Goslin. The man's face was suddenly blank again.

"Ethnic bias?" Lenczi's rather thin but penetrating voice rang out and he pushed irritably at the drooping eyeshade as he smiled with wry amusement at the accusing student. "Oh, come now. What a thing to accuse a Hungarian of!"

"How can you deny the bias in your statement?" the student bellowed.

"My dear Mr. Sullivan, there was no bias in my statement. It was a matter of fact and statistical—"

"Statistics only prove what you want them to prove!"

Lenczi smiled tolerantly. "Submit your own statistics, Mr. Sullivan, and we'll program the Mark IV with both sides. Surely even you must agree that a computer is unbiased."

"Only if it's been programmed by an unbiased mind."

Lenczi threw up his hands, appealing humorously to the gathering that this was a lame rebuttal.

"Shall I inquire of IBM how many Negroes—excuse me, blacks—were employed to construct their computers? Or shall we insist that it be programmed to answer in Swahili or Ashanti rather than Astran?"

"Good heavens," murmured Berstock, "he's good at rebuttal, isn't he?"

"Now, just a moment, Lenczi . . ."

Lenzi's thin figure jerked straighter and the student's moment lengthened into a half-minute of silence. "I expect," Lenczi said in a cold voice, "to be addressed as Doctor or Professor, Mr. Sullivan. Now, if you will excuse me, I have my lunch to complete and a class at one."

He shut the window firmly and turned away. The group fell to arguing among themselves, none of them observing the arrival of Rentnor, Berstock, and Goslin.

"Jack Sullivan, you're a fool!" a girl was saying. "He's a mathematician, not a racist. He's made it plain that he based his opinion on mathematical fact, not emotional garbage. Do you people have to distort everything to suit your ends?"

"Who do you mean by 'you people'?" Jack Sullivan demanded in a hard, belligerent tone of voice.

Rentnor now placed the T-shirted, long-haired student as a sociology major, a sometime opponent, sometime cohort of the Breslaw Hall alliance.

"By 'you people' I mean the hysterical destructionists who are interfering with my right to an education!"

"Your right? You've a lot of gall, Susan Anderson, demanding *your* rights, *your* selfish individual rights, when the rights of a whole race have been denied them."

The girl, pretty, blonde, intense like so many of her generation, laughed in his face, an ugly derogatory laugh.

"I'm paying for my education. It's not being handed me because I'm black and that's the 'in' thing. I earned my right to get into this so-called institution of higher learning by damned hard swatting at books, by working for higher grades. And I resent—" she was a nose away from Sullivan's face in her fury—"I resent being deprived of my math course because Professor Lenczi made a statement of pure, logical fact."

"You're all alike, you damned Wasps!"

"Ahha!" The girl threw back her head, her blonde tresses whipping into Sullivan's face. "There, you've labeled me, Jack. Happier?"

Then she plowed her way through the group and into the Math Building. There was a spate of murmurs, private agreements and dissents, while Jack Sullivan glared after her retreating figure. As he turned back to the others, he saw Rentnor and his companions.

"Atten-shun!" he cried loudly and derisively as he assumed an exaggerated military stance. "The brass approaches. Trying for another government contract, Rentnor?"

"Aw, shut up, Sullivan," someone said, and most of the students, embarrassed by his blatant insolence, nodded or smiled or said good day to their president. There was an immediate exodus until only a nucleus of four students, three whites and a coffee-skinned boy, remained around Sullivan. They glared defensively as Rentnor escorted Berstock and Goslin inside the Math Building.

It was cool and almost too quiet inside the dark hall. Rentnor glanced out again and noticed that Colvano and his group had joined Sullivan's.

"If you don't mind, Dr. Rentnor, we'll wait a moment here. I don't like the tone of that young man's comments."

"Neither do I!"

Berstock nodded understandingly and then gestured to Jeremy. The moron's face was suffused with hatred, his nostrils flaring. "We got him in just in time. Now, Jeremy, it's all right. Project reassurance, Dr. Rentnor."

Not exactly certain how to comply, Rentnor smiled vigorously and was absurdly put in mind of Mary Martin adjuring two small children to think happy thoughts while she was hoisted about the stage on a flying apparatus. However, Jeremy's excitation shortly vanished.

Berstock peered outside, jerking back as the reinforced group crossed the paving and moved to the left, out of sight.

"They're clearly up to no good and, but for Lenczi's firm handling, this might have exploded into an unpleasant episode." Berstock sighed. "I've come at a critical moment, I fear. We'll just let them get out of range and then I'll follow with Jeremy. We may still be able to forestall a full-scale riot here."

Rentnor reached for his bleeper. "Shall I . . ."

"Oh, definitely not." Berstock stopped his hand. "We can't have the uniform of authority on hand. Only inflame them. Please. Find out exactly what they were saying to Professor Lenczi before we arrived."

Berstock smiled encouragingly at Rentnor and urged him toward Lenczi's office.

"Yes, I'd better find out what was said, hadn't I?" Rentnor was quite suddenly obsessed with a desire to know.

Lenczi, munching happily on his garlic sausage and bun, was unperturbed by the incident.

"Piff! What they want is impossible. A black mathematician represented on the Math faculty. If there were one qualified, I would accept him instantly. Hungarians can work with anybody. We've had practice." Lenczi gave a snort at the historical exigencies of his native land. "Of course, I didn't tell them that the main stumbling block would be lack of finances to support the salary of an additional mathematician." Lenczi had been pleading for an additional instructor for several years. "Of course, they don't want this man, this black mathematician who doesn't exist anyhow because other universities have acquired all the qualified men already, as an instructor. Oh, no!"

Lenczi gestured wildly over his head. "No, he must be at least an assistant professor. Nothing less is good enough! Ha!" He took a savage bite out of his sandwich. "Do they appreciate at all what is involved in attaining such academic rank? No! Faugh!"

"And that's all they're after?" Rentnor was somewhat relieved. Cavaye couldn't be faulted if no candidate applied. And if advertising such a vacancy would pacify the radicals . . .

"Of course not!" Lenczi replied so forcefully that some of the garlic sausage and bun accompanied his words from his mouth. He nodded an apology as he patted his lips with a rather soiled tea towel. "Don't be obtuse, Dr. Rentnor. The impossible is only the first wedge they wish to insert in our ivy-covered halls so that you, me, all of us, trip over it."

Rentnor felt a wave of terrible apprehension and depression drenching him.

"What can you expect, Rentnor?" asked Lenzci in a mild, semi-amused way. "It is spring." He waved toward the closed window behind him. "And since young men's fancies no longer turn to thoughts of love in this permissive age, they must think of rebellion. It is a logical progression of the human equation of these times."

"How can you be so . . . so calm? You'll be the target."

Lenczi shrugged. "That's not a new condition for me either. But they are only talking at the moment. And there were as many young people for me as against me. Mathematically, statistically speaking—" and Lenczi grinned with total amiability—"the odds still favor Papa Lenczi." He brushed some crumbs from his shirt. "It was kind of you to come to my rescue. But I was well in command of the situation. There are surely more important things for you to see to, Dr. Rentnor."

There was more than a trace of irony in Lenczi's manner, Rentnor decided as he rose and shook hands with the Hungarian. Rentnor vowed to do something about Lenczi's interminable requests to replace the ancient blackboards with the more modern green which reduced eyestrain. He wondered briefly if Papa Lenczi would continue to wear his green eyeshade, so much a fixture of his college image. Rentnor was wondering whether he'd touch the Contingency Fund for those greenboards or the unrestricted grant from . . .

He was almost to the door when the ominous sound of a crowd penetrated his financial reflections. He stopped just as the first wave of students came marching up the pathway. For one brief moment he hoped they were just passing, but as they inexorably turned toward the building, more and more students were swelling out behind the vanguard in a solid threatening mass. Rentnor ducked into the nearest classroom, fumbling for his bleeper.

"MacCrate, what's happened? How did that mob start?"

He could barely make himself heard over the noise as the students swarmed into the Math Building. He could hear them thudding on Lenczi's door.

"D'ya want us to close in, sir? We're all ready," shouted MacCrate.

"Come on the run! Call the city police!"

Sounds of breaking wood, of shattering glass punctuated the angry shouts and bellowed instructions. Suddenly the door into Rentnor's sanctuary burst open and the overflow from the hall spilled in.

"Stop right there! What's the meaning of this? Disperse!"

"It's prexy himself!" snarled Jack Sullivan, pushing to the fore. The man radiated hatred and anger. And as he stood there, his hatred and anger appeared to intensify in him, in the faces around him, in the steadily mounting tempo of destruction which pulsed in this congregation of once pleasant, placid, innocent children. Only Rentnor's cool defiance was keeping them at bay. If he'd just a few moments in which to divert their . . . Rentnor's mind was rapidly churning through the possibilities, scanning the faces of the first ranks, hoping to find one possible ally in their midst.

And saw . . . the unbelievably altered countenance of Jeremy Goslin. In horrified fascination, Rentnor watched as the moron panted with an increasing passion of the anger, the hatred, the vengeance so vividly reflected in his suffused features. Rentnor watched, immobile, as the contagion of those violent emotions began to ripple convulsively through those nearest Goslin, until the aura preceded the eruption as a shock wave precedes the noise of a bomb.

"Goslin!" Rentnor cried, pointing at the moron. "Him! He's an outside agent. A paid agitator! A Marxist! *He's* the rabble-rouser."

Rentnor's timing was off by a split second as Goslin erupted through the mob toward Rentnor, the object of an incredible, telempathetical broadcast that had turned the dissatisfied but orderly students into an unthinking instrument of destruction.

As Rentnor tried to evade Goslin, as he was buffeted by the students swarming over him, he thought less of the indignity and pain than he did of the ignominy of inviting the enemy, Berstock, right into his campus and helping him prime the mechanism, Goslin, who could turn his campus into another riot-disaster arena.

And when tempers had as suddenly cooled and the students had departed or been evicted from the shambles to which the Math Building was reduced, it didn't surprise Rentnor that there was no trace of Berstock on campus nor of Jeremy Goslin among the broken heads and teargassed victims.

Discreetly he checked with Berstock's university, to be told that the Doctor was on a sabbatical leave, doing research among the natives on a South Pacific atoll relative to their growing legends about nuclear tests in their pacific vicinity. The secretary remarked that there seemed to be more interest in contacting Dr. Berstock when he was on sabbatical than when he was actively lecturing at the university. Rentnor asked whether there had been a Jeremy Goslin connected with the Doctor.

"Good heavens, no. He wasn't *with* us," said the woman curtly. "After those experiments were finished, he was sent back where he belonged."

The records of that institution showed that Jeremy Goslin had disappeared. The police had found no trace of him. Since he was incapable of fending for himself, he was presumed dead.

The quickly suppressed riot on a small Southern campus did not make much in the way of headlines. The ISACA and Vibeke committees made no mention of it when they visited Cavaye.

When Rentnor read articles about other previously quiet colleges erupting into unexpected violence, he wondered if Berstock and his rabble-rouser had been active again. He might have tried to warn against this vicious task-force, but he was in a position where such a course would be an error in judgment. It could be misconstrued by the money-giving agencies which insured Cavaye's academic future.

Rentnor took out his frustration at another level. He expelled nineteen students, suspended forty, ordered the murals painted off the students' hall, and had the college architects work on plans for subterranean installations.

the serpent in eden

poul anderson

Regardless, the planet was beautiful.

Even as the aircraft bucked and shuddered, caught in the hurricane shriek, Janne Granstad remembered Cleopatra seen from space. Against night and stars the globe had glowed, blue with its oceans, green, gold, and umber with its lands, swirled silvery with its clouds. The brighter light of the whiter sun made those hues at once more vivid and more serene than Earth's, whose loveliness had always lured tears out upon her lashes. And then the diamond sweep of the ring!

Outside the windows, blackness and lightning raved. Violence toned through metal and bones. The craft lurched insanely, threw her against her seat harness till straps dug into flesh. Arch Fielding turned his head around from the controls. She could just make out his cry: "No use. We haven't got the ceiling to get above this stuff. I'll have to ride it out till—" Janne lost the rest of his words.

She thought, dimly astonished: *That shouldn't be. Should it? No storm should be that tall. But, of course, we aren't on Earth, Earth is nearly 400 light-years south of here. . . . No, wait, "south" doesn't mean the same any longer, Cleopatra doesn't have the same lodestar. . . .*

Roberto de Barros leaned across the narrow aisle between their seats to take her hand. That was almost more bewildering. Or was it? He gave her a stiff smile and said amidst the fury, "Don't be afraid. This is a stout vessel. While we stay aloft, we are safe."

Are we? Janne asked in dread. At once: *No, I must not panic. We have too many unknowns around us to conjure up needless ones. The laws of nature are the same here as they are at home, or in the farthest galaxy. Only the parameters are changed. And not very much. We can live here. We can walk unarmored beneath a sky and breathe an air men have never befouled, we can wash our bodies inside and out with the purity of waters, we can taste the fruits of an untainted soil. Earth today may be more alien to man than is Cleopatra.*

But don't think despair of any kind. Think prose, think science. Her mind almost chanted: *The F7 sun gives us a third again the terrestrial irradiation, a higher proportion of it in energetic particles and quanta. The lower gravity, 0.86, means air pressure dropping more slowly with altitude. The rotation period is less too, seventeen and a third hours, making stronger Coriolis force. The smaller size of the planet may be a factor, bringing climatic zones closer together. And how many more variables have we overlooked? No wonder storms are big, wild, and so unforeseeable by us that this one actually caught us in flight.*

There was courage in the dry recital. But the weather ramped on, and on, and on, driving the aircraft helpless before it.

And when at last clouds broke, sunlight speared through, wind faded as swiftly as it had arisen, Fielding told his companions in a stark voice: "We've gone on too long. Fuel's about finished. I'll have to set us down on the first decent-looking ground I spot."

Peering through the pane beside her, Janne made out crags tumbling toward endless forests. But on the horizon, the sun low above, glimmered what had to be ocean. Then they'd crossed this whole small subtropical continent, caught in the westward half of the cyclone. Base Island lay 2000 kilometers behind. The magnitude of that struck her like a blow.

De Barros said, "Don't be reckless, Fielding. Husband your reserves. Don't descend unless we are all three positive it is safe."

"Shut up," the pilot snapped. "I'll be the judge of that."

De Barros grew rigid. "I think you are exhausted and overwrought," he said. "Granted, you are the most experienced flyer, but not at present the best. Let me take over."

"No!" Fielding yelled, and threw a curse after it.

"Or Dr. Granstad might," de Barros suggested, as if she were not on first-name terms with both men.

Janne shrank back in her seat. "Don't," she whispered. "Please. I—I'm sure Arch can—"

"I was thinking mainly of your welfare," de Barros told her, but had the wit to pursue the argument no further.

Janne took refuge in watching Caesar sink, red and gold, toward the sea without a name. How small the sun was. Or—wait—it was farther away than Sol is from Earth. Otherwise Cleopatra would have been scorched barren. By day one didn't notice the size of the disk—who could look near it?—but when coastal haze gentled its brilliance, the horizon illusion exaggerated the difference—

"Hang on," Fielding said over his shoulder. "Pray if you want. And if we don't make it . . . Janne, I'm glad to have known you."

He gave himself back to his flying. The craft slanted downward. A wide sandy beach appeared in the forward panes, grew with terrifying speed, leaped and struck.

The vehicle bounced. Teeth rattled in jaws. Across hundreds of meters, their dunes and tricky little airs, Fielding brought his machine to a halt.

When peace had thundered upon them, Janne would have flung off her harness and kissed him. But he twisted his neck to confront de Barros and said nastily, *"That's* how come I didn't want you at the console."

De Barros shocked her himself when he replied, cool-voiced, "My compliments on your good luck, at least. Does it extend to establishing communication with Base?"

They knew it did not.

Night was unreined sorcery.

The strand glimmered white, the wilderness behind lifted cupolas of darkness against stars and remote snow-peaks, the ocean before played a million sparkles, light-ripples, glades, and the huge broken ring-image across its ebony. Waves rolled *hush-hush-hush,* the ever gentle surf of Cleopatra. Breezes were mild, bearing alike the smells of salt reaches and green growth. Sand was still warm underfoot, fine enough to yield like flesh caressed. Somewhere, something unknown trilled a song.

Stars glistened in the middle heaven as if to crowd out a black which itself felt luminous. Meteors went among them, streak after silent streak. Northward they were lost in leaping banners of aurora, white, blue, violet, ice green, and ghostly rose. Southward soared the ring. The dust, gravel, and stones which had once been a moon had become a wan rainbow that reached a third of the way up the sky, along which trafficked hasty, flashing, and tumbling jewels in their hundreds. At this season, early winter, the shadow of the planet did not quite scoop out the middle of the arch; the ogive it made was almost visibly rising as night moved onward.

And then lifted Charmian, the larger of the two fragments which men had found worthy of a name. Was the name worthy of her? However tiny, at her nearness she showed as big as Luna seen from Earth. She was less bright—hardly even a globe, rough, scarred, changeable as she spun, though often a scoured spot of metal caught a sunbeam and flared—but she did not have to shine through city fumes and glare; she kindled the waters.

At their edge, Janne roused from her watching to think, guiltily, that she ought not to have wandered from the men. She could see them, distance-dwindled, as they began setting up camp. The glow-stove became an abrupt crimson star. She noticed she was hungry. *Why didn't they call me*

*to come do my share? I drifted away because it seemed
they'd be fiddling with the radio and squabbling with each
other for hours yet.* In pain: *Why must they, here in a
miracle?*

She started back, a tall and limber young woman, yellow
hair chopped off below the ears and coverall carelessly
worn, but her body possessing the handsomeness of good
structure well tended. Being at the core a practical person, as is the duty of any explorer, she answered herself:
*Well, it's not a miracle without its troubles and dangers.
They're under strain, Arch and Roberto. We could die.
That doesn't seem likely, in this moment's majesty; but
what will we find tomorrow, or what will find us?*

She knew there was no foretelling. A planet is a world,
infinite in the number of its faces and mysteries. The fifty
people whom *Hanno* had brought were the first who ever
saw Cleopatra. Before them, nothing except a robot vessel
had made that enormous journey and returned to report its
discoveries. They amounted to little more than the fact of
an orb which seemed to be habitable and uninhabited.
Machines can only find what ignorant men have programmed them to find.

And in the weeks since arrival, the expedition had barely
begun to learn. The data which observers aboard the
orbiting ship could gather were valuable but lean. Those
who went down and established themselves on Base Island
had studied it, and the mainland shore opposite, with
fanatic intensity; but they had necessarily concentrated
on things like the chemistry of rocks and life, rather than
topography or natural history. This flight was among the
first intended to go farther inland. It was supposed to
fare some few hundred kilometers, descending here and
there for a closer look, returning within three or four days.
Instead . . .

Janne shrugged. Wryness twitched her mouth upward.
*We named you better than we knew, Cleopatra. Lovely
but—hm—capricious.*

Fielding, who had been hunkered over food prepara-
tion, rose as she approached. Though everyone was now
too used to the lesser weight to notice it, he, who had been

a trifle awkward at home, was graceful here. He was a
lanky man with a bush of black hair and features she
thought were good-looking in their broad-nosed, deep-
brown fashion. They had found much in common on the
long voyage hither, after they saw it was best to set political
differences aside. He remembered with pleasure a visit to
her Norway; it was less ruined than most of Earth, he
said. She had studied in his North America. Their pro-
fessions did not really sunder them either, he an engineer,
she a naturalist; nobody on this trip could afford to be
narrowly specialized.

"Hi," he said. "Want to take over cooking? Short
rations need a woman's touch."

"Short?" she asked.

Fielding jerked his head at de Barros, who was raising
the tent. "He insists. Says we may be stranded for quite
a spell."

The Brazilian left his own work to come and say, "It
is an obvious possibility." As always, his slender form
was neatly outfitted and soldierly erect. Upon the thin-
sculptured head, prematurely gray hair and mustache had
gone argent in this light. His English was less fluent than
the others', but he spoke it when with them, rather than
the official Portuguese or Japanese of the expedition. Janne
didn't know whether that was a gesture of friendship or
of condescension. Perhaps it was one toward her, another
toward Fielding. In spite of the North American's radi-
calism, she felt she understood him; both their countries
remembered not only having once been prosperous and
democratic, but having once been satellites of nobody else.
Aristocrats, however, were outside her experience, whether
baronial Brazilians or magnates of the New Empire.

"You mean," she asked, half timidly, "the radio inter-
ference will keep on for long?"

"I am not positive," de Barros admitted. "Our knowledge of stars like Caesar is less than complete. Still, storms
upon them have been seen to remain at peak for as much
as two terrestrial weeks. Until the present one diminishes,
no transmission of ours will carry all the way we have
come from Base."

His redundant last sentence made Fielding scowl at what could be a subtle insult. But as if to emphasize, the auroras suddenly flamed high and lurid. The shadows they cast danced across the beach. Janne gasped in awe.

"We are too small to be located from space, and only two of the aircraft have ample range to get here and back, *if* our whereabouts are known beforehand," de Barros continued, likewise unnecessarily. "Hence we must wait till we can send a message and, I suppose, have fuel brought us. It seems common sense to stretch out our food supplies."

Fielding's hand chopped at the forest. "When we've got a whole continent and ocean full of eatables?" he scoffed.

"Are you sure it is?" Janne cautioned.

"Why shouldn't it be? Life uses the same basic stuff everywhere on a planet. And conditions on this coast don't seem especially different from the east."

"You're assuming a great deal, Arch."

For an instant Janne feared that Fielding would gibe at de Barros with something unspeakably obvious of his own. Perhaps: "Yes, I understand that while similar environments have produced basically similar biochemistries on two planets, the parallelisms couldn't be exact. Cleopatran flesh and fruit lack some of the compounds we must have, like certain vitamins; and a proportion is turning out to be poisonous to us. This has its advantages. It works both ways. Cleopatran diseases can't get a foothold in us. And we *can* supplement our diets, deliciously, if we're careful."

But instead the North American gave her one of his full-lipped smiles and said, "Right. I know what close relatives the potato, the tomato, and the deadly nightshade are. Don't worry. I won't eat anything you haven't certified as a type we checked out on Base and proved was safe. I am betting we'll find a lot hereabouts."

Though such identifications were part of Janne's job, she felt unhappy at the responsibility. Seeking words to explain, she turned her gaze outward, along the shining beach. What she saw made her go taut.

De Barros noticed. *"O que há?"* he exclaimed.

"Shhhh." She pointed.

A hundred meters away, a creature had stepped from the forest onto the sand. Light shimmered off a tall, thin, eerily manlike body. It halted, crouched bent-legged, and peered at the strangers.

She heard a slither as Fielding drew his gun. "Don't shoot," she whispered frantically.

"*I'm* playing it cautious, no more," he assured her. "Damn, isn't that something!"

All personnel went armed. Thus far there had been no need for it, except to collect specimens. Janne had been glad of that; and, necessary and fascinating though dissections were, she hated seeing slain animals brought to her laboratory shack. It reminded her too sharply of whale and elephant, stag and lion, every kind of wildlife much bigger than a rat or a roach, which Earth knew only in archives. Yonder one, erect, alert, brought back to her some chimpanzees she had once seen in a film . . . O God, almost human faces, faunlike awareness behind the eyes. . . .

Frozen, the forest dweller watched them.

De Barros was first to move, charily, back to a pile of gear. Janne glimpsed him draw forth a pair of night glasses and bring them to focus.

She had never before seen him shaken.

"*Madre santa!*" burst from him. He dropped the binoculars. She snatched them up for herself. The animal sprang into clear view.

Startled by the noise and movement, it was loping back to cover. In its left hand—not paw, hand—it gripped a rock shaped and edged by what must be chipping.

It vanished. Charmian, entering the shadow of the planet, turned dull coppery-red.

At dawn Janne again strayed off by herself and stood looking over the sea. It had awakened to a million blues and greens, white-laced where waves met land. Out upon some reefs basked scores of great long-necked marine reptiloids. Their numbers bespoke how rich in life these waters must be. The sky, cloudless, was already too lightful for the ring to show, except for a swift phantomlike Iras, Charmian's half-sized companion. But it was not empty, that sky. Thousands of wings shared it with the sun. Clamor drifted down to meet the low surf noise.

Shadows were long, more blue and sharp than on Earth. The air was brisk, barely on the cool side of balmy, laden with fragrances which mostly were different from those of sunset or night.

"Good morning," said de Barros.

Janne turned to greet him. Immaculate, he offered his usual slight bow. "Did you sleep well, since you have risen this early?" he inquired.

"No, I was too excited," she said. "But I don't mind." Impulsively: "I can't get over the—the abundance here. The whole horizon seems bigger." It wasn't in fact, she knew. The equatorial diameter of Cleopatra was 9920 kilometers, 78 percent of Earth's, which meant that, under present conditions, she could see about one kilometer less far.

He surprised her by saying, "It is." After a moment: "This marvelously clear atmosphere. Vision isn't caged by pollution. Perhaps I could show you something comparable on our estate in Rio Grande do Sul, the grasslands. . . . But no." He shook his head. "They are an enclave which will last no longer than our family's wealth and power. Meanwhile, every wind brings filth." He sighed. "Here on Cleopatra—Janne, I begin to understand why my ancestors worshipped the Virgin."

What? she thought. *Is the aristocrat baring his soul?* And then: *No. I shouldn't be sarcastic when he's trying to be friendly.*

It wasn't the first time, either, she recalled. De Barros had found occasion after occasion to talk to her. That wasn't easy. Besides his being a planetologist, a scholar of rocks, magmas, inanimate forces, there was the lack of privacy on Base Island. No two people were ever far from others; it might not be safe. *And, well, Arch has been particularly likely to interrupt.*

"You've seen several new planets," she said, for lack of better words.

"None like this," de Barros answered. "They had their wonders, but men could never make a home on them. A world where we can live, truly live, is more rare and precious than we can well imagine. It is like being given Eden back, to try again."

"Do you think people might colonize here?" It had often been speculated about, but the general feeling was that Caesar was too remote from Sol, at the end of too long a haul. It would never be possible to ship very many emigrants, and they would be more isolated than ever were Pilgrim Fathers—or Greenland Norse, who died out.

"Oh, yes, indeed. Let them see our account, and those who can will sell whatever they possess to buy a one-way passage and barely enough equipment for a start."

"But . . . cut off . . . and the uncertainties, the dangers . . ."

"Janne, I can name you a good many persons who would not mind in the least being cut off from our present excuse for a civilization. I rather suspect I am among them. As for danger, in a very few more generations Cleopatra at her worst will be safer than Earth at her best."

"You can't think that: you!" she blurted.

De Barros shrugged. "I am a scientist, who abhors politics and the military. But coming from the family I do, I cannot avoid noticing things, including things the public is not to be told. We are far closer to a far more serious ecological crisis, and the international balance of power is far more precarious, than the insiders admit even to themselves."

Janne winced. "How I hope you are wrong."

He cocked his head. "Forgive me. I didn't mean to distress you on such a gorgeous morning. Let us therefore simply speak of adventure, opportunity, freedom, healthful and beautiful surroundings. Consider yourself. You stand so raptly watching those animals. There must be work for a hundred lifetimes of naturalists. Would you not be happier here than anyplace else?"

Janne bit her lip.

"Why are you sad all at once?" he asked low, and took her arm.

"That being," she got out through a thickness in her gullet.

"Ah. The tool-bearer."

"Yes. I did daydream about pioneering, when it didn't seem Cleopatra had intelligent life. But now . . ."

"Marvelous in truth. To be sure, what we saw appeared less developed than man."

Janne shook her head. "I got a pretty good look at the hand ax. It's made as well as specimens from Earth's Paleolithic were . . . by Homo sapiens. Oh, perhaps you can't teach calculus to the maker. But perhaps you can. And even if not, his breed must be on their way, well on their way, to becoming as bright as we are—their own kind of consciousness, which surely can't be the same as ours."

"You wish to learn more about them, do you not?"

" 'Wish' is a feeble word. I was afire until—Roberto, are you certain colonists will be coming?"

"Yes, if we don't discover some terrible obstacle."

"Maybe we can."

He considered her before saying, "You are afraid that man, permanently on Cleopatra, would destroy the aborigines."

"I am. Think what he did to his fellow men who were weaker, or to the dolphins and apes. I could hope he'd have the sense to learn from Earth and use a new planet right. But don't you see, whatever he did, he'd be *using* it. Making it his, changing it, dominating. . . . He might grant natives a few wretched reservations. No more. What then of their own dreams, everything they might have done, might have given to the universe? No," Janne said through tears, "I don't want to be a party to that. How could I ever dare die?"

She fought for calmness. De Barros ventured to lay a hand on her shoulder. "Easy, easy," he murmured. "You are borrowing trouble. Let us first learn the facts—whatever we can—seeing that we must be here for a while anyway. You have never had a more fascinating challenge, have you?"

"No," she confessed, and felt a surprised gratitude that he should be this understanding. *He's really a good person,* she thought.

"Uh-hum!" said Fielding at their backs. "For your information, I've found where the nearest fresh water is. So how about you making breakfast?"

The men matched fingers to decide who should accompany Janne on her first excursion, and who guard camp. Fielding won; at any rate, he seemed to regard it as a victory. De Barros philosophically said he could study a nearby outcrop. Cleopatran petrology had its duplications of the terrestrial, but already at Base he had discovered differences which a geologist would call spectacular.

The other two collected their equipment. While not planning to go far, they carried compasses—the planet had a stronger magnetic field than Earth—and small transceivers—the electrical chaos in the upper atmosphere wouldn't stop short-range radio, if one didn't mind static. In addition, they bore weapons, first-aid kits, Janne's professional tools, and a couple of sandwiches.

Travel was simple—no tangled brush to fight. Cleopatran plants did not seem to have evolved as far as angiosperms, at least on this continent. However elaborated, they were basically primitive, mostly soft-bodied and disinclined to grow in dense masses. The chief exception was an intensely green stuff which resembled moss (and wasn't), making a springy carpet underfoot.

Janne recognized some of the vegetation. In various cases, she had helped devise the names. Several dinobryons were in sight, upheaving their great spongy masses like coral knolls. A dichtophyte had stretched its network between two of them, strands ranging from cable-thick to thread-fine for the entrapment of animal prey. Metallic particles in the leaves of a Venus mirror made them sheen; the bush was surrounded by insectoids whose wings were similar, and Janne guessed it attracted them to pol-

linate. Nestled beneath the outward-bristling spearpoint
stalks of a sarissa, a chameleon plant shifted hue as il-
lumination changed. There were many more kinds of
rooted life than these, a few suggestive of ferns, lycopods,
fungus, or evergreen trees, most wildly exotic. Besides
every possible shade of verdure, the forest had its bursts
of vivid red, purple, yellow—not true flowers, but poin-
settia-like pseudoblooms.

It was warm and quiet here, a checkerboard of bright
openness and sun-speckled shadow, a multitude of odors
sweet, pungent, pleasantly rank. Most of the abundant
animals were small and not noisy. Insectoids buzzed or
hummed. A swarm of smidgins passed, the tiny individuals
merged into a cloud; two leathery-winged reptiloids flapped
along, leisurely feasting. A jackadandy flaunted plumes of
a sort, though it wasn't a bird either, and trilled. The largest
beasts seen were half a dozen hipposaur, grazing at a
distance. But Janne was utterly charmed when she came
upon a reptiloid new to her, likewise a peaceful herbivore.
It could afford pacifism, being a two-meter-wide walking
dome of bony armor and spiky tail. "We must call that
a hoplite!" she said, clapping her hands together.

"Huh?" Fielding asked. "It doesn't look as if it could
even hop heavy."

Janne laughed. "An infantryman in classical Greece.
Roberto was telling me, several days ago . . ."

"Oh. I'm afraid my education's been neglected. Come
on; if you want to search for natives, we should keep
moving."

His sourness drew a troubled regard from her. "What's
the matter, Arch?"

"Ah, hungry, I guess. That stupid rationing . . . No,
that isn't really it. I think you can see what is."

Her cheeks heated. She decided not to reply. They
walked on for a number of minutes.

"Okay, damn it, I'll speak out," Fielding said. "It's
that Brazilian bastard, and you getting chummy with
him."

"I know you'd overthrow his class, his entire country
—and you know I don't agree that violent revolution ever

improved anything—but, Arch," Janne pleaded, "we're human beings together, a long, long way from home."

"He hasn't left *his* interests behind. You can bet your blood he's figuring how his relatives can get a stranglehold on this planet—squeeze out the Japanese, sure, but make peons out of the settlers—"

"He isn't! We've talked—"

"Yeah, he wants you in his bag also. Janne, you may be a little naïve, but you're not stupid. You know the signs."

I do, sighed within her. *Inescapable, perhaps. We aren't many women along; and I*—her fingers knotted together—*I'm one of the few who are neither solidly attached to a man nor available to a lot of them. . . . The psychologists should have picked the crew more carefully. Did they try and fail? It must be hard to find qualified volunteers among Earth's poverty-trapped masses.*

Fielding stared before him as he tramped and added harshly, "I suppose you've seen them on me too."

"You—you're sweet," she stammered, "but—"

"But not just what you're after? Who is, then? A rich Brazilian? I'm not sweet at all. I can be as mean as necessary to keep him from getting you."

Janne bridled. "Arch, you're overstepping."

"No. I'm worried sick. You don't understand how rotten his type is. Why, I'd rather see you the mistress of Captain Yoshida than the wife—the toy, the slave—of—"

"Nok! Enough! You're making me understand why Roberto loathes fanatics. Stop slandering him before I stop liking you."

He swallowed. They continued, through a land where she could no longer find beauty.

But after more minutes a new sound broke the silence between them. They halted, strained their ears, stared at each other with anger forgotten. Janne's heart leaped. She beckoned Fielding to follow her, well behind; she could move more quietly than he.

A screen of something like tall bracken rose in front of the clattering. Janne crept up to it, parted stalks and fronds, peered through.

What I thought! What I both hoped and feared it would be.

The creature squatted in a glade where a ridge of flinty rock thrust above soil. It was a reptiloid, hairless; small scales were darkly iridescent in the sunlight. Erect on clawed feet, it would overtop her by a few centimeters. The frame, unobscured by clothes or ornaments, was manlike in a sense. Its alienness—lean barrel of a torso, long, curiously jointed legs, short arms and the way they hung from the shoulders, slender tail—did not make it grotesque; this body had its own grace, its own integrity. The neck was likewise long, flexible, supporting a narrow head. The eyes were its best feature, large and golden, protected by arching ridges that, with the membranous crest on top, made the skull resemble an ancient helmet. The face was flat, a single nostril slit in place of a nose, mouth V-shaped in a perpetual grin, jaws of nearly human delicacy. When they opened, the variety of teeth indicated that here too was an omnivore.

Here too were hands. They were not hominid. Instead of a thumb, four claw-tipped fingers radiated in a half-circle from the palm. But they worked as well. The Cleopatran was making a *coup-de-poing.*

Janne had studied a little prehistory. She recognized the technique. A bone held in one hand struck pieces off a chunk of rock which the other gripped. The labor went fast, in clash and sparks. The resulting outline would be like a thin spear, pointed, sharp-rimmed, about twenty centimeters in length. It would be an all-purpose weapon and tool; the user could throw it to knock down small game, or cut, crush, flense, butcher, scrape, slice, carve. When it grew dull, a new edge was easily put on; when it broke or was lost, a replacement was quickly made. Shards heaped on the pseudomoss showed that generations had used this site.

Hand axes, scarcely to be told from the one taking shape, had been found throughout Earth's eastern half by the many thousands—man's main reliance through tens of millennia.

Man: the tool-bearing animal. Then how can we deny the spirit yonder?

The Cleopatran raised its head and stared. Its tail switched. Fielding joined Janne, his gun held steady. A single explosive bullet could blow the stoneworker in two.

"Don't shoot," she breathed.

"If it acts threatening, I will," he answered. "You're worth more than any glorified snake."

The Cleopatran rose, hefting the almost finished ax and the bone shaper. Despite herself, Janne tensed to duck. However, the being merely regarded them. A breeze brought its musky odor.

She held out her open hands. *"Vi er venner,"* she said. At once the humor of stating "We are friends"—in Norwegian!—kicked a giggle from her, half hysterical.

"He can't know we're not some funny kind of beast," Fielding muttered. "In fact, we are."

"Until we communicate," Janne replied. The thought flitted: *Yes, let's say "he." Cleopatran life has two sexes like ours. I'm not sure which this person is, but "it" isn't right.* She stooped, with an idea of scratching patterns in the ground. The being retreated, vanished in brake and shadows.

"Cautious," Fielding opined. "After all, we're two to one. Maybe he figured you were about to throw a flinder at him. Or maybe he's gone after his buddies. I think we'd better head straight for camp."

Reluctant and disappointed, Janne nonetheless had to agree. She rose and they began walking. "I don't expect they'll be hostile," she argued. "Why should they? The lower animals don't fear us; they've never learned to. . . . Still, I could imagine—well, being trampled by a horde of eager curiosity-seekers."

"Or whatever. I'd feel more trustful if they were mammals."

"Theroids," Janne corrected automatically. "There don't seem to be any true mammals around, just primitive little animals that don't even lactate."

"A cold-blooded, egg-laying thinker. . . . It feels wrong." The engineer grimaced.

"Why? Remember, the reptiloids of Cleopatra—many of them—are further evolved than reptiles on Earth. They have efficient hearts, for instance. I suppose the planet's being warmer, probably never having had an ice age, gives less relative advantage to homeothermic over poikilo- thermic organisms, so the latter have had more chance to develop onward."

"Homeo—huh?" Fielding scowled. "Never mind. I admit to being prejudiced in favor of mammals. You, no doubt, consider this the most wonderful thing we could have found."

"Of course." Janne hesitated. "Or the most dreadful."

"How that? You don't imagine men have much to fear from a bunch of savages, do you?"

"Yes. They have to fear what they'll be tempted to do." Janne told him her forebodings.

His air of distaste turned to one of reined-in-fury. "And de Barros encouraged you in that sentimentalism? I guess I shouldn't be surprised. It'd make a nice additional excuse —protecting natives—for aristos to keep their feet on settlers."

"What do you mean, Arch?" she exclaimed. "That men should come and . . . take their world away from these people . . . destroy them?"

"If need be. When you've seen, lived with, slum chil- dren whose faces were gnawed by rats—and I have— you won't let a bunch of scaly, lipless *things* stand between them and a chance at a decent existence." After a moment: "Oh, I don't advocate extermination, unless we must. We can maintain preserves."

It scarcely eased the horror in her. She had nothing to say while they returned.

Their route was different from before. Near the coast Fielding halted. A stand of dactylophytes, looking like fleshy shrubs, glowed golden-green. "Hey!" he said. "Pork- plant!"

Janne roused from her mood to answer, "Or a close relative."

"Well, for heaven's sake, let's collect a bundle and come back after more. Now our bellies won't growl."

Analysis and experiment on Base Island had shown that the fronds were tasty as well as nutritious to man—not a complete diet, of course, but a welcome supplement.

"I don't know," Janne said. "We haven't a biochemical laboratory along."

"Why should we need any, for this? Sure, first you put a sample under your microscope and check if it's the exact same species, free of parasites or whatever. I'll bet you a month's pay you'll report positive."

"I wish you wouldn't eat it, Arch."

She failed to dissuade him. In camp, she found he was right about the classification. Nonetheless, she refused a share. De Barros smiled wryly and said, "You may guess whether or not I am disguising cowardice when I declare that if a lady is to go hungry, so will I."

Fielding, his pleasure dashed, glowered at them and grumbled, "Well, at least one of us will keep his strength up." At dinner he feasted ostentatiously.

Next morning a Cleopatran appeared on the beach. It wasn't the same as yesterday's, being of lesser size and having only a rudimentary crest. Janne guessed it was a female, while her previous encounter had been with a male. The creature carried a hand ax of her own. She poised a distance from the aircraft and, when Janne drew slowly near, hissed and made as if to cast the weapon. Janne halted. They exchanged stares for a minute, until the girl tossed a gift of porkplant. The Cleopatran took it up, ate it, and sidled back into the forest.

To de Barros, who had guarded her, Janne remarked, "They really are shy, aren't they? I suppose they think we're supernatural."

"Let us do the traditional thing," the Brazilian suggested: "set forth some trinkets for the next visitor."

Having brought none, they improvised, deciding what could be sacrificed in the way of bright cloth, buttons, a hand mirror, a diffraction grating. It was fun. Janne wondered if they might not be a touch light-headed from hunger, they laughed so much. No, she concluded; it was de Barros' considerable stock of dry humor. The pangs weren't bad, just a continuous reminder that she had a stomach. Tight rationing was not the same as starvation.

It struck them that colored polaroid photographs should make ideal gifts, and they went about looking for good subjects. Fielding found them at that.

In well-fed vigor, he had gone off to try his luck fishing. (The proper word, "ichthyoiding," was unlikely ever to become popular.) His catch had been abundant; one needed merely drop a hook or sweep a net through these swarming waters. When he saw Janne and de Barros side by side, composing a picture of pseudoblooms, he flung his creel at her feet. "There you are," he snapped.

"What do you mean, Arch?" she asked uncertainly.

His gaze smoldered. "I wanted as many different new species as I could snag, for you," he said. "Seems like you'd rather hang around camp playing games."

"That isn't fair," de Barros protested. "We are trying to establish communication with the natives."

"Yah, yah, yah." Fielding stalked from them.

Janne spoke in pain: "That isn't like him."

"He does not care for me," said de Barros.

"But he's never been this . . . childish."

"Let him sulk."

The enjoyment was gone from her undertaking. She and the planetologist finished it, though, laying forth their offerings at the spot where the Cleopatran had twice emerged (if it was the same they had spied the night before last). Thereafter they waited. Fielding ate a big lunch, and later sought his sleeping bag for a nap. That wasn't characteristic either.

The return of the being drove concern about him from Janne's mind. The slender, sheening form trod daintily from behind the dactylophytes. Grown less wary of aircraft, tent, and humans, she stopped, peered their way, and neither retreated nor threatened when Janne advanced. "Hasn't she seen our presents?" the girl wondered aloud. She tossed a chunk of porkplant in among them. The

Cleopatran promptly went after it, picked it up, and stuffed it in her mouth. When no more was forthcoming, she wandered on down the beach. Bewildered, Janne and de Barros stared after her.

Abruptly she must have noticed signs, for she squatted. Sand flew beneath her scooping hand ax. Soon she reached into the hole she had made and drew forth some equivalent of a clam. With the tool she pried it open and severed meat from a shell. Having eaten, she returned inland.

Man and woman did not speak for a long time.

"I've *got* to learn more," Janne said, over and over, that evening. "Track our visitor down to her community or . . . or whatever we find. It'll be safe, I'm sure. They've been gentle, even timid. But don't you see, this is an impossible paradox, toolmakers who ignore new artifacts. If we don't come to understanding of it, who knows what surprises may be sprung on us—back at Base too? Besides, as short of manpower as the whole expedition is, we have a duty to use what time we're bound to spend here."

De Barros opposed her going herself. In the end he yielded, on condition he accompany her. She was much the best suited for such an investigation. He adapted a portable gas detector. Given a fresh scent—the natives left a strong one—and duly adjusted, its meter needle was as good a tracker as the bloodhounds of history.

Fielding had said little, except to complain that he felt poorly. During the night his illness rocketed.

A sound of vomiting roused Janne. She hastened from her bag and out of the tent. Under stars, meteors, ring, and aurora, Fielding crouched on the sand. He heaved and shuddered. When she laid arms around him, she felt sweat upon an icy skin.

"Roberto!" she wailed. "Wake up, help, help!"

Between them, they got the North American cleansed and brought back into shelter. By the light of their flashbeams, his eyeballs rolled white. Lips pulled parched away from teeth. "Here," de Barros said, "here is a cup of water."

"Not from you," Fielding mumbled. "You poisoned me. Or she did. Lied to me . . . so I wou'n' connerdic' whatever lie she'll tell 'bout this planet to save her damn snakes. . . . Murderers, both o' you—"

Dawn walked russet over the mountains. Waves glittered and whooshed beneath a salt breeze. Winged life went aloft in its thousands.

Outside the tent, where Fielding lay in feverish sleep, Janne and de Barros traded looks. "You didn't believe what he accused me of, did you?" the man rasped.

"Of course not." She shook his hands.

"I am not . . . ruthless. Neither are my kinfolk. He sees us as tyrants and schemers. He cannot see troubled people trying their clumsy human best to cope with a worsening world."

"I can, Roberto. I don't think your way of coping is always right, but your good will I've never doubted—nor that of the Japanese." In a rush: *"I'm* the one who poisoned him! I told him those plants were probably safe."

"If that is the trouble."

"What else could it be? And they seemed so—so identical in every way with—"

De Barros frowned and chewed his mustache. "Precisely. I admit to thinking you were overcautious, and only followed your example because— *Bem*, never mind why. Don't blame yourself. You did your best, short of telling him a falsehood. Besides, it may well be something else. He may have picked up an infection. We have not absolutely proved that no indigenous germ can affect us. Or he may have been exposed to a factor that we were too, but had an idiosyncratic reaction. Without intensive clinical study, there is no telling."

"Then there's no treatment." She swallowed hard.

He nodded. "Nothing but supportive treatment, and prayer that his body can throw off the effects by itself."

"We have a whole damn pharmacy along."

"But what drug to use?" de Barros reminded her. "What antibiotic might work on a Cleopatran microbe?

Or if this is an allergy, do we want antihistamine, anti-
venin, or what? If it is an organ-specific toxin, which does
it attack and what is the antidote?" He clenched his fists.
"We dare not medicate on a guesswork basis. Most drugs
have side effects. We could too easily touch off a syner-
gism, where between them the disease and the 'cure' kill
him. And while this radio blackout lasts, we can't even
get professional advice."

"How does he seem to be doing—honestly?" Janne
made herself ask. As a venturer onto several different
worlds, de Barros had acquired a good deal of practical
knowledge.

The Brazilian's tone bleakened further. "Not well.
Pulse, respiration, temperature, nausea, diarrhea, and
the resulting dehydration . . . he is sinking."

"O God, O God." Janne almost cast herself upon his
shoulder. But instead—she didn't quite know the reason—
she went off to weep alone.

The native came back.

Janne, huddled on a rock, was first aware of it when
sand scrunched. Looking up, she saw the neat dino-
saurian shape close to her, ax loosely held, mouth smiling
wide as if in anticipation.

"Why—why, Cleo," she stammered, and scrambled to
her feet.

The other being stood a minute longer. Receiving no
food, she turned and departed. Her stride took her right
over the gifts which lay, gaudy and forgotten, on the shore
of the sea which had no name.

It struck through Janne: *Couldn't I follow, observe?
It may not be entirely wise to go alone. Still, anything's
better than waiting useless for Arch to die.*

She hastened to fetch the sniffer. De Barros had barely
noticed what went on. Hands caught white-knuckled behind
his back, he paced in circles around the tent. His face
seemed well-nigh as haggard as that of the unconscious
man within.

"I'm going after Cleo," Janne said.

De Barros surfaced from his broodings. "No, you mustn't without a partner, and we can't leave our comrade."

"One can tend him as well as two for a short while. I'll be careful. There isn't any danger, really. I can't get lost in those open woods, with the sun for a guide. If I should be attacked, besides my gun, I have my legs. I can outrun any reptiloid." In a surge of gallows mirth: "Remember, nature designed me to weigh ten kilos more than I do here."

"Nevertheless—" De Barros broke off. It was as if suddenly he no longer saw or heard her.

"I won't be gone long," said Janne hastily into the silence that she took for consent. She hurried off in pursuit of the native. Once she cast a glance behind. The Brazilian stood motionless, staring out over the ocean.

She wondered briefly what had entered him, but dropped that question in the excitement of the chase. Though Cleo had disappeared, where tracks in sand met vegetable mat, the detector needle pointed straight inland. Movement was swift through that parklike forest. Presently she saw the being's head bob and sway above a row of fronds.

Cleo glimpsed her in turn and halted. For a dizzy moment Janne thought, *Maybe at last she'll give me a sign.* The creature wandered on. Frustration tasted harsh in Janne's throat. She followed at a discreet distance.

Why do they all but totally ignore us? Maybe they believe that's how to treat gods or demons. . . . No. They've been careful about us, but not frightened. She took food from me. Why did she spurn our other offerings?

Cleo drifted in no special direction. She dug up and ate a sugarroot. She spied a small theroid on a branch overhead and cast her ax. It missed; the animal scuttled off; she retrieved the weapon and continued her stroll.

Where is the male we met? Where are any more whatsoever? . . . Oh!

Cleo stopped dead. Her tail stiffened. Out from a clump of bushes, jerky, jaunty, shining in sunlight, came a young one of her kind. It could be nothing else, a miniature, half a meter tall, carrying its own doll ax. *The darling!*

Janne screamed.

Cleo had hissed and hurled. The baby saw. Barely in time, it sprang aside, wheeled, and fled. Cleo bounded after. She grabbed her weapon on the run. Stems bent, branches snapped. Jaws agape, she bounded in chase.

Horror roared around Janne.

Comprehension exploded it. She sank to the ground and shrieked forth laughter like a woman gone crazy.

Caesar, blazing its rapid way across heaven, stood to westward. The ocean flashed gold above sapphire, turquoise, and arabesqued alabaster. Sands shone, forest glowed, snowpeaks lifted in purity. Wings rode upon crystalline, flowing air.

In that hugeness, vehicle and camp seemed flecks which a stray wind had blown in and would soon blow away again forever. Janne's heart twisted when she saw how de Barros had erected instruments to observe the sun. *Poor haunted man, he needs his own place to hide,* she thought, and quickstepped toward him.

Yet, spying her, he dropped the screen on which he had been projecting a magnified disk. He ran. His hair tossed gray and wild. He grabbed her to him and kissed her. "Janne, it worked, it worked!" jubilated in her ear. "Already he is conscious, clear in the brain, *sim,* he has a little strength and—you did it, you, you, you!" He let her go, save for taking her hand. "Come. He would like to see you."

In the yellow dimness of the tent, she knelt by Fielding's bedroll and sobbed for joy. He gave her a shaky smile. His voice was still barely audible. "Hi, honey. Want to cook me a bowl o' soup in a while? You pick the recipe."

"You are getting well?" It was a stupid question, but she had just been snatched out of anguish.

"Yeah. Ol' Doc de Barros thinks I'll be on my feet in three-four days. Now that the poison's leaving me, I can take cell stimulants and . . ." His mien turned anxious. "Janne, can you and . . . and Roberto . . . ever forgive me?"

"For what? You were sick, dear Arch." She brushed lips across his. "What you can do for us is take care of yourself."

"I obey. I've learned. From here on in, I listen to you." Fielding uttered a chuckle. "Funny. Eden . . . forbidden fruit . . . this time the man tasted, 'spite o' the woman. . . ." His words trailed off.

De Barros touched her. "Come," said the Brazilian. "Let him rest. It is a natural sleep."

Outside, she drew breath after breath until at last she could say levelly: "Then it was the porkplant."

"Well, yes and no," de Barros replied. "You gave me the clue."

"Me? How in the universe?"

"Granted, a chance remark of yours. However, I have an idea that chance favors those who deserve well. When you were running off—do you remember what you said to me about your weight on Cleopatra?"

"Um-m-m . . . yes, since you mention it . . . but what—" Janne sat down on a dune and hugged her knees. "Tell me."

He joined her. "It triggered something," he explained. "Perhaps I would have gotten the thought anyhow, but probably not in time. Arch was failing fast. I was desperate enough to try anything, if only I could find the least clue.

"Well. Cleopatra is smaller than Earth, therefore its gravity field is weaker. But that weakness is not in proportion. If the two planets had the same density, we would weigh less here than we do. And, actually, if they had the same composition, Cleopatra should be somewhat less dense, because of a smaller mass compressing itself less at the core. In fact, the mean density is ten percent *more* than Earth's. This must be due to a greater proportion of heavy elements, as the spectrum of Caesar also indicates. Doubtless this whole system condensed later than Sol's, from a nebula which had had time to accumulate more large atoms. For Cleopatra, that means more radioactivity, a hotter interior, hence the outgassing of as much atmosphere as we have around us—" De Barros shook himself. "I babble. You know all this. I too am a little silly from happiness."

"Go on," she urged.

"You recalled the fact to me," he said. "I realized that there must be surface regions where heavy elements happen to be especially concentrated. There are on Earth. Plants in such areas may take up the metals and become toxic. For example, locoweed—selenium-contaminated desert forage—is a menace to livestock. I heard about that from a bailiff on our estate. . . . If this can happen on Earth, how much more often on Cleopatra?"

Janne straightened. "By glory, Arch's symptoms did look like arsenic poisoning, didn't they? Now that you've pointed it out!"

"I am not sure what element is responsible," de Barros said. "Perhaps several. A broad-spectrum chelating drug did the—ah, did the trick."

He paused before continuing: "I have found that the solar storm has passed its maximum. I estimate we can get a call through in about six more days—C-days, that is. Therefore we can give Arch adequate nourishment without starving ourselves too much—" he grinned—"or resorting to organically grown foods."

"Splendid," said Janne absently. Her mind had gone elsewhere. "Animals must have an immunity, whether or not a given soil is metal-bearing. The possibility will be a hazard for humans. Not too bad. It simply means people must check a region before they settle in it, and take what precautions are indicated."

Surprised, de Barros said, "What? Have you resigned yourself to colonization?"

Janne laughed. "Goodness! I'm sorry, Roberto. Your news made me forget I haven't told you—or Arch. He'll be so glad. In spite of his . . . his ideas about human supremacy . . . or his dislike of 'glorified snakes' . . . I can't believe he was really single-minded about us overrunning a whole other sentient race."

"Wait a minute." De Barros seized her arm. "Do you mean the Cleopatrans are *not* intelligent?"

She nodded. "I should have deduced it earlier. Besides the youth of this world, its generally primitive biology, there was the toolmakers' absolute lack of interest in communication, lack of curiosity, lack of community. My guess is, they're solitary. Individuals stake out territories, sharing the flint sources. Male and female meet just in mating season. Yes, I should have realized they aren't thinkers, long before I did. What clinched it was seeing a small one fending for itself. Consciousness demands learning, which demands parental care. The lowest mammals and birds look after their young. Cleo . . . The moment she saw this hatchling, she wanted to eat it."

De Barros sat appalled.

"It escaped," Janne said. "Don't be shocked. I was at first, till I realized what the significance was. They're as unconscious, you might say innocent, as fish or praying mantises."

"But they make tools!" he protested.

"That was what blinded me too," she replied. "We know we evolved with tools in our hands. Naturally we supposed that whatever other kind of life uses them must be like us, or at least like our near ancestors."

She sighed. "The truth is," she continued slowly, as if to herself, "we're unique, on our planet, only because we've destroyed our brothers. In that moment I remembered what I'd read or seen filmed from long ago when they lived: a sea otter pounding an abalone open against a stone he held on his chest: a beaver colony damming a river; a chimpanzee shaping and wetting a straw to catch termites with. . . . At that, we still have termites, and the other ants, and the bees. They still do things which are much more complicated than chipping stones into one particular shape.

"Not that these—what shall we call them? Fabers? Not that they aren't wonderful, and important, and with many truths to teach us. How I hope the people who come will spare them."

She rose, walked from him, gazed out across the sea to its clear and burning horizon. "Eden," she finished. "We are the serpent."

beachhead in utopia

lloyd biggle, jr.

Coming from the board room with a stack of papers, Miss Philp said plaintively, "It isn't enough that it's E-day and also the end of the month. *They* want the annual report released today."

Miss Rodney rippled a stack of data cards, fixed her myopic gaze on Miss Philp, and asked absently, "What was that? Oh. E-day and the end of the month aren't what snarls things up. It's the board meeting. As the members walk in they suddenly remember all the things they were supposed to do between meetings but didn't. Research is in a turmoil."

Miss Philp sniffed. "Research goes into a turmoil whenever anyone asks a question. They think they're being imposed on if they're asked to work one day a month." She seated herself at the voicewriter, donned the microphone, and said grumpily, "I'll be dictating all day. The board'll revise every page six times."

Mr. Helpflin, of the Records Section, looked in at them, nodded, asked, "Has Mr. Dorr been here?"

"He's at the meeting," Miss Philp said.

"I didn't know they'd started. Is there any way to get a message to him?"

Miss Philp smiled coyly. "There might be—if it's important enough."

"Fellow downstairs wants an interview."

Miss Philp sniffed. "Is it about an extension?"

"Well—yes."

"He's on today's list, too, I suppose."

"Yes."

"Tell him every case is reviewed by the full board before finalizing."

"In my opinion, the fellow deserves some consideration. Is there any chance at all that Mr. Dorr would see him?"

"No chance at all," Miss Philp said firmly.

"Do you have his name and number?" Miss Rodney asked.

Helpflin glanced at a slip of paper. "William Zarny. F-97-043-15."

"I'll look him up. If Mr. Dorr happens to wander through here, I'll tell him the case interests you, and I'm sure he'll see that the board takes a careful look at it. I won't promise anything, though. Usually Mr. Dorr stays in the room until the meeting is over, and if anyone interrupts a board meeting, it'd better be important. I mean *really* important."

"This is *really* important—to William Zarny," Helpflin said grimly.

"If *you* want to take the chance—"

"No, thank you. If you see Mr. Dorr, please tell him about it."

He left with a nod and a smile, and Miss Philp sniffed again and loaded the voicewriter's feed hamper with masters and duplicating sheets. Miss Rodney was flipping through a stack of files, and when she found the one she wanted she opened it and drawled, "Well, wouldn't you know!"

"Know what?" Miss Philp asked.

"William Zarny. He had the full two years of training,

and he didn't do a lick of work for the next two years plus three extensions."

"That's what I figured. I mean, I thought the F list had been liquidated. Three extensions is as many as the law allows, isn't it?"

Miss Rodney nodded. "I'll tell you this much—I certainly wouldn't mention *this* case to Mr. Dorr. Zarny's one of those slobs who figures society'll support him in grand style for the rest of his life, and suddenly it's E-day and he's used up his extensions. An interview with Mr. Dorr—indeed!"

She hunched her shoulders resignedly and began matching data cards with files. Miss Philp threw a switch, took a deep breath, and began to dictate. *"International Poverty Control Agency, United States Branch. Tenth Annual Report. It is with understandable pleasure that your National Poverty Control Board announces new and dramatic progress toward a goal that seemed unattainable only a decade ago: the total elimination of poverty from our midst. Occasional setbacks, such as the failure of a major industry during the past year, have been taken in stride. . . ."*

Her voice droned on, expertly inflecting the chirps and grunts to which the machine's punctuation marks were attuned.

William Zarny entered the first bar he came to and ordered a drink. The bartender took his credit card, glanced at it, glanced again, slid it into the register, and touched a button. He returned it with the drink, remarking, "Expires today."

Zarny nodded. He downed the drink with one gulp and marched away.

At the Christian Unity Center he entered the Protestant offices. The receptionist smiled at him. "Back again?"

"They said I might see Bishop Corlett today."

"Zarny, isn't it?"

"William Zarny."

She flipped a switch. "Do you have a William Zarny on Bishop Corlett's list?"

The flat answer came a moment later. "No."

"Whom did you talk with?" the receptionist asked.

"Mrs. Warren."

She flipped another switch. "Mrs. Warren, there's a William Zarny here. He says you told him—"

"I couldn't work him in," Mrs. Warren answered. "Tell him to come back tomorrow."

"Today is my E-day," Zarny said desperately.

"Today is his E-day," the receptionist said. "He's been coming here for months. Isn't there someone—"

"Send him up. I'll see."

Mrs. Warren indicated an interview room, and after a tedious half-hour wait an owlish-looking young man walked in, nodded, took the seat across from him. "I'm the Reverend Walter Kammity. Something I can do for you?"

"I hoped someone here might be able to find me a job."

The Reverend stroked a smooth cheek thoughtfully. "There are four governmental agencies and I don't know how many private ones—"

"I've tried *everywhere.*"

"I see. Well, Mrs. Warren will give you a card to fill out, and—"

"I filled one out months ago. And today is my E-day."

"I see. Why did you wait until the last minute?"

"I've been trying to see Bishop Corlett for months."

"We aren't exactly in the employment business," the Reverend said reproachfully. "And the Bishop is a very busy man."

"I'll do *anything!*"

"That's what they all say—on E-day. You should have been willing to do anything a year ago."

"I was. I've done nothing but look for a job for almost three years. They gave me special training, you see, and then . . ."

"Then they couldn't find a job for you. Most unfortunate, but those things happen."

"Anything at all . . ."

The Reverend shook his head. "The law is the law,

you know. Sometimes the welfare of society requires measures that impose sacrifices on individuals. I'm sure that none of us would want to return to the old system, where poverty bred crime and more poverty, and children grew up in an environment of material and spiritual degradation and extracted revenge by preying on their fellow men for the remainder of their lives. By keeping the welfare lists at a minimum we're able to give an unemployed worker's family a respectable standard of living and maintain that until he's had ample time to find employment, but even in these prosperous times we can't support indigent families indefinitely on that basis. If we didn't establish a cutoff date and enforce it, in a very short time the old tragic cycle would be operating again."

"I don't care about myself," Zarny said desperately. "But my kids are bright, and if they had half a chance . . ."

"You've had two years of training, you say, and then two more years plus whatever extensions you were allowed. That adds up to almost five years, which was surely ample time in which to give them a chance. Have you told them?"

"No. I didn't want to. . . ."

"Did you send them to school today?"

Zarny nodded.

"It's best that way," the Reverend said approvingly. "There's no point in worrying the little ones about something that's beyond their control. I've seen some utterly shameful scenes result when the parents thoughtlessly told their children. Well. All I can do is express my regret and assure you that, compared with the old system, this is much, much the better solution." He fumbled in a pocket and laid a token on the table. "I'd suggest that you stop in the chapel on your way out. This will give you two free prayers in the Meditation Alcove—wait. You still have your credit card, don't you? Then you won't need this." He pocketed the token and opened a memo book. "William Zarny. Wife's name? Children and ages?" He scribbled the information. "I'll include you in my devotions tomorrow. No charge for that, of course. Good morning."

The receptionist glanced at Zarny's face and said, "I'm sorry."

"Thank you for trying," Zarny said.

"I wonder—I've heard that Father Wilks has had some success at finding jobs. Just a moment." She telephoned, asked a question, thoughtfully replaced the receiver. "He does find one now and then, but he has a waiting list of his own parishioners."

Zarny nodded and said with a wistful smile, "Thank you. I probably won't see you again."

He headed up the street toward the Municipal Employment Office. He'd been there every working day for more than two years and he knew that he didn't stand a chance, but he wasn't ready to face his wife and children. Not yet. Not until he had to.

Mr. Helpflin met Mr. Dorr in the corridor and asked, "Did Miss Rodney speak to you, sir?"

"About what?" Dorr asked.

Helpflin consulted his slip of paper. "William Zarny. F-97-043-15. He's on today's E-list."

"What about him?"

"It's rather complicated. Somebody made a colossal goof, and he's paying for it."

"What sort of a goof?"

"Well—he was an expert computer technician. The old General Data Corporation's M1095. It's obsolete now, sir, and as fast as it was replaced with advanced models the 1095 technicians found themselves out of work."

"Happens all the time," Dorr said cheerfully. "Why didn't Zarny train on one of the advanced models?"

"He did, sir. That is, he thought he did, but when he finished he couldn't find employment. He's been trying, really working at trying, but—nothing. I first heard about it this morning, and it sounded fishy to me."

"I should say so. Computer technician is a demand occupation."

"So I checked his record. His two years of training were put in on the 1108—which was obsolete before he finished. No wonder he couldn't find work!"

"I see," Dorr said thoughtfully.

"And he isn't eligible for another training course until he's worked for five years."

"It was the Training Center's goof," Dorr said. "Let *them* straighten it out. They can waive the five-year requirement for cause, and their own goof should be cause enough. Get in touch with them now, and if they'll accept him for more training, we can grant him an extension."

"He's already had the maximum."

"Well, we can waive that for cause, and his acceptance in a training program would be cause enough. The board has broad powers of discretion, you know. It doesn't use them impulsively, but it won't knowingly liquidate a man who's potentially useful. It'll be meeting the rest of the afternoon. If you can work something out with the Training Center, get word to me right away."

William Zarny left the fourth employment office. He'd skipped lunch; he hadn't felt like eating. He had two choices left—to go home and wait, or to go down fighting. He chose to fight. He went to a car rental agency, where the clerk looked at his credit card suspiciously and remarked, "Expires at five o'clock. Got a renewal?"

Zarny shook his head.

"E-day, eh? You wouldn't be thinking of taking your family and skipping, would you?"

"How far could I go on an expired credit card?" Zarny asked bitterly.

"What do you want the car for?"

"To look for a job."

"Did you apply for an extension?"

"I've already had the maximum."

The clerk said thoughtfully, "Just a moment." He called to the clerk at the next window, "Wynn, weren't you saying something about some unemployed guy who finagled ten extensions?"

"Sure. Why do you ask?"

"This fellow has used up his extensions. How was it managed?"

"Special case," Wynn said. "Guy'd been disabled in

an industrial accident. Something about his spine. The doctors were confused and kept thinking maybe he'd be able to work again. It was medical extensions that he got. Eventually the doctors decided he was a hopeless case, so—no more extensions. They took him and his family last E-day."

"This fellow's E-day is today. He wants a car to look for a job."

"A little late for that, isn't it?" Wynn asked.

Zarny did not answer. He was tired of explaining about those two years and nine months of searching, and applying, and waiting in anterooms, and arguing with secretaries and receptionists, and filling out forms and data cards that would be filed and forgotten.

"Sorry," the clerk said. "I just can't take the risk. I don't want to lose my job. In this occupational class, one bad-judgment mark and I'd be on my way to E-day myself."

"I understand," Zarny said. "Thanks."

He turned away, more resigned than resentful. It hadn't been a good idea anyway. He had little time left, and he shouldn't be wasting it driving around. Outside, his gaze focused on the massive, ugly tower of the Federal Building—which, as everyone knew, had more computers per unit of floor space than any other building in the city. He headed that way, walking quickly.

Miss Philp, grumbling that they meant to keep her there all night, began dictating page seven for the fourth time. She reached the bottom of a column of figures and paused for breath. Miss Rodney was sorting through the next group of files. A messenger entered and handed her an envelope, and she glanced at it skeptically. *"Mr. Dorr —Urgent. Deliver immediately.* I'll bet." She opened it. "William Zarny again!"

"What about him?" Miss Philp asked.

"Something about his classification. It can't be all *that* urgent, but it's not my neck. Helpflin signed it. Still, just to be on the safe side—why don't you take it in when you have the next pages read?"

The receptionist said firmly, "I don't have to check. We haven't had a call for that job code for years."

"Please check anyway," Zarny said.

She shrugged. "If you insist. But I know—" She broke off as a light flashed. "Yes, Mr. Brakely?"

"Have you found anyone who can service a 1440?"

"No, sir. I've checked all the employment services, and—"

"Get on the phone and borrow a technician from someone. We're already a week behind with the tax statements, and the whole third floor is sitting around waiting on that dratted machine."

"I'll try, sir." She buzzed off.

Zarny swallowed and asked, "Is that a GDC1440?"

The receptionist nodded.

"That's my machine!"

"No." She shook her head emphatically. "Yours is the 1108."

"I should know. I had two years of training on the 1440!"

"Let's see your classification card again." She snapped it into a machine, read off the code, opened a classification manual. " 'A' means you're a class-one technician, 'G' is for General Data Corporation, 'K' means the 1100 series machines, 'D'—"

Zarny stared at her. "I never knew that. I mean, they gave me the card, and I just assumed— No wonder I couldn't get a job!"

"You actually trained on the 1440?"

Zarny nodded. "Trained on it for two years, and they've sent me their modification specifications ever since."

"Then someone punched your master card wrong," the receptionist said. She pressed a button. "Mr. Brakely? I have a man here—he has the wrong classification, but he claims that he trained on the 1440s."

"We'll soon find out," Brakely growled. "Send him up."

"Any reply yet?" Mr. Helpflin asked.

"The memo just went in," Miss Rodney said.

"But I marked it *urgent!*"

"So how urgent is urgent?" Miss Rodney asked.

Helpflin glanced at the clock. "Those who've had extensions are always processed first, and he's had three extensions. He'll be one of the first ones taken."

"So? It's only four o'clock."

"That leaves just an hour, and I don't know how long it takes to process a cancellation."

"What's all the fuss about?"

"This fellow trained on the latest-model computers, but someone made an error in coding his classification. His data card makes him an expert on an obsolete model, so of course no one would hire him. Now that his classification has been corrected, he can go to work anywhere. They tell me downstairs that two 1440 technicians are needed in this building and they'll hire him this afternoon if he'll apply." He glanced at the clock again. "I'm going in there and straighten this out now."

"It's your funeral," Miss Rodney muttered, but Helpflin marched away. He was back again two minutes later, triumphantly waving an official cancellation card.

"Now all I have to do is find a messenger, and— No. I'm taking this over to E-headquarters myself."

"A short circuit in bank ten," Zarny announced.

"How long will it take to fix it?" Brakely demanded.

"I've already fixed it."

"The devil! And you say you've been out of work— how long?"

"After I finished retraining, two years and nine months."

"Those idiots!" Brakely said disgustedly. "But why didn't you catch the error yourself?"

"You can't tell that a card is punched wrong just by looking at the holes," Zarney said. "Even if I'd put it on a machine, that particular code wouldn't have meant anything to me without a manual. And no one ever said, 'We don't need anyone for our 1108s.' They always said, 'We don't have any openings in your classification,' and naturally I assumed that they were referring to the 1440s."

"Everyone needs 1440 technicians," Brakely said. "I'm

putting you on the night shift. See how many machines you can have operating by morning."

"Yes, sir. But this is my E-day, you see—"

"I understand. I'll take care of that. You concentrate on those 1440s."

Miss Rodney and Miss Philp, starting their second hour of non-compensated overtime because they could not leave until the board adjourned, had their boredom relieved momentarily by a clash between Mr. Helpflin and Mr. Dorr.

"We issued a cancellation," Dorr said. "I handed it to you myself. What'd you do with it?"

"I delivered it in person."

"So what's the trouble?"

"You didn't grant an extension. They crossed off his name, but the minute his time expired the master E-computer issued a warrant for him."

"I see. We didn't think about that—busy day, you know."

"That warrant overruled the cancellation. Without an extension it had no legal validity. Zarny's wife and children were picked up on schedule and taken directly to the ovens. In the meantime, the fellow got himself a job—"

"Really? Good for him."

"His employer sent in the information and a request that he be removed from the E-list. Because he wasn't home when the E-squad came for his family, a warrant had been posted on him. He was eligible for E-treatment on sight because of the expiration. As soon as his boss's message hit the master computer, the computer dispatched a squad to pick him up at his place of employment. Imagine that—arresting a man on his job and hauling him away to be exterminated because he's unemployed!"

"Did they get it straightened out?"

"Of course. The error in his classification has been corrected, and he's been removed from the E-list because he's now employed. But he and his family are still dead."

"So why did you call me out here? There's nothing *we* can do about it."

"I called you out to tell you that the board is going to have some explaining to do. The man's employer was the Federal Government, and the local office is suffering from an acute shortage of computer technicians. The office manager is threatening to demand a Congressional investigation."

"That's easily taken care of," Dorr said blandly. "Give him a priority and find the technicians he needs. Until you do, loan him one of ours." He turned to Miss Philp. "A few changes in this page, please. These are the last, I promise. We're down to our final order of business."

He hurried away. Helpflin stonily headed in the other direction. Miss Philp flipped a switch and donned the microphone. *"Because of the low unemployment rate and the anticipated continuing reductions in joblessness, this branch of the Poverty Control Agency will be able to cut its staff immediately by twenty percent. Further personnel reductions of at least an additional thirty percent should be possible during the coming year, with a resultant savings—"*

Miss Rodney gasped, "What was that?"

Miss Philp looked up in surprise, turned off the voice-writer. "I wasn't paying attention. I could dictate in my sleep, and after a day like this I probably am. Cut its staff . . . further personnel reductions . . . *oh!*"

They stared at each other.

The board's final order of business.

Dismissal notices.

geraniums

valerie king and barry n. malzberg

ROOTS: Dmitri was no one's fool. The world was going mad, but he wasn't. Not that way. He knew a geranium thief when he saw one. And there she was, sliding up the walk. God, they were cunning!

Cunning, cunning! It was hard enough to coax the plants along the asphalt, past the clay, without these constant thieving forays. The rectory was stone, he was earth (he thought of himself as brisk, mud-covered perhaps but always brisk), but how could you win? And there was the religious overlay too. He had never thought he would end up among Catholics. Maybe the geranium thieves were demented and the cunning was something that he credited them with only because one wanted to see, *had* to see the enemy as personal. . . . Nevertheless, in a eucalyptian crouch (the branches wavered) he shook with rage as he watched the bitch. All of them had the same gait: mince with the shopping bag dangling from an arm, the other free to deftly snatch a plant. They were pure evil; the rectory could have its snake. And yet, rage or not, he would stand in something close to anticipation (all right; he *identified*) watching the ritual of movement: the hand would shoot out between the fence grillwork and snip a stem or two, then the explosion of bloom. *Slam!* into the bag backhand and then the mince again. Up the path and across the street. You had to admire them. They knew what they were doing.

This lady, he supposed, was a new one. Maybe not; their faces blurred like flowers. New or old, though, the thieves worked the same: limp, sweep, snatch, stagger . . . and then he saw her back as she moved sedately down the street. Her shoulders trembled. She was laughing at him.

Hilarion was no help. Father Hilarion thought the thing was delightful. "Geranium thieves!" the crazed old celibate would say, his eyes glazed with passion or holy water. "A parish of geranium thieves! Well, Dmitri, one must share blessings earthly as well as un-." And so forth. "What's so bad about a few miserable geraniums? It could be the roses!" He hated the man.

Dmitri saw Hilarion stumble from a side door and come toward him clasping a rosary, then, at the exact moment when he thought communion was about to be offered, Hilarion swung north and followed the geranium thief up the path. Dmitri turned on the sprinkler. From this new aspect Hilarion disappeared into shining mist, a rainbow, in the center of the rainbow a potted plant.

STAMEN: In the last two years dreams of his childhood had overtaken him. At the beginning it had only been once a week or less, the dreams interrupted by a heightened apperception of what was happening to him now, but the tempo had picked up: now they were coming almost all of the time and in the dreams there was a succession of fat women in black dresses, talking to him inexhaustibly, lifting, sweeping, stirring, and passing on advice in a language he could not understand. Isolated phrases—*humming; persist; consider the lilies*—would sweep in, connect, but they would lapse to jargon and he would bolt from sleep, swearing. He could not understand what they were trying to tell him. Lying on his back, sheets to his knees, he would imagine himself to be looking not at the miserable gardener's ceiling but a wedge of pure sky, rain falling.

In the dreams his childhood accumulated. He had not been sensitive to it the first time around, but now it was all coming back, the ethos of it, so to speak, the realization that it had all somehow been quite painful. Obviously he was going to get all of it back if only the women would open up and speak comprehensibly. The dreams, furthermore, had been coming on him recently during the days, stroking at him like wind in the dust of the garden. He found himself locked into recollection and came from it to see that time had passed and once, through the window, he had seen Hilarion waving at him with the lazy strokes of a carnival wheel.

PISTIL: Dmitri had made sure to put the Empress of Russia in the center of the garden. Safe from the hands through the fence. The Empress of Russia was a miracle; the black-purple blooms had the texture of velvet. It proved that the apocalyptic Catholics were fools.

All of the thieves were after his Empress of Russia. Of course they were. But Dmitri, like the Apostle Paul, had drawn the line: some things were theirs and some were not. The ladies might snatch a geranium but no more, not by vaulting the fence or a more subtle attack.

Shutting off the sprinkler, Hilarion down the path, Dmitri worked ten minutes or more, clearing a shallow basin beneath the tangerine tree, sneaking little glances now and then at the Empress. All right, he should have married or at least worked for a non-sectarian institution. It took him a while to realize that he was being watched.

He rose and looked at the lady. She was the same one who had been there before. Green pedal-pushers. No shopping bag this time. "Isn't that beautiful?" she said and pointed to the Empress. "Give me a snip. Just a little one off to the side where it won't show."

Dmitri went to the Empress, broke off a stem and, going to the fence, handed it to her. "It won't work," he said pointlessly. "Won't work at all."

"That's the only one I wanted," she said. She looked

at him and she was one of the ladies in his dream and little insect eggs of understanding became larvae through him. Aristocracy. Of course! The stout ladies with their perpetual cleaning and lectures were part of fallen aristocracy. Like the Empress of Russia. Of course.

"Actually," the woman was saying, "I'm not a Catholic, unfortunately. We're Methodists, pretty lapsed, but Catholicism is so *persuasive*. Flowers from stone and all that."

"Get out of here," he said.

"Yes," she said, "yes," and cupped the Empress; walked away. He put his hands on the fence and watched her.

PETAL: "You're handling this all wrong," Hilarion must have said to him. "If you can't bear to give away cuttings, why do so? Pretend you're deaf. Turn your back."

"They're evil."

"Evil," Hilarion might have pointed out, smoothing his robes, "does not have anything to do with flowers."

PISTIL: Later he must have returned to the basin. Late afternoon now. His digging had uncovered a gopher hole, and looking into that darkness, Dmitri had an insight: he dragged a hose to the basin and turned it on full. Then he shoved the hose all the way into the hole. Water came out of the hose, turning the basin the colors of the rainbow. Never had he felt so much in control. The nozzle should go *all* the way into the hole, he thought ponderously; that way the gopher, if it was still there, would certainly drown. He slammed it in so deeply that the stream departed. Dmitri understood what the women in their black dresses had been trying to tell him. They had not liked the cheerless atmosphere, that was all. Something to brighten it up, perhaps, Dmitri? They had been talking about flowers.

A small and dark thing came out of the hole and bobbed in the water. Dmitri fainted or imagined that he did.

Hilarion was beside him, in full dress. "What's wrong?" he asked. He extended a hand, from the hand a flower. "Tell me, my son," he said. *Son.* Dmitri was fifty. More of their mysticism.

Dmitri looked up. Hilarion seemed to be of an enormous height, at a great distance, shuddering over him, hand extended. A gopher, the old fool was saying. Dmitri had caught a gophher. Wasn't that nice? It showed that the rectory had life in it.

He rose. He looked beyond Hilarion to the clusters of geraniums. The Empress blossoms were bruises and he became aware of a fine, spidery aching within his chest. God, he needed water.

He was pulled upward. The hose was taken from him. Waving, Dmitri opened his arms to the sun. He waited. In due time a hand would snake through the fence, draw him out like wire, and take him toward Ascension.

In the background, Hilarion seemed to be chanting the *Kyrie*. The old fool. They understood nothing. There were no mysteries. The world was a greenhouse.